THE LAST OF DEEDS

THE LAST OF DEEDS

EOIN McNAMEE

Raven Fiction

Raven Arts Press/Dublin

THE LAST OF DEEDS
is first published in 1989 by
THE RAVEN ARTS PRESS
P.O. Box 1430
Finglas
Dublin 11
Ireland

ISBN 1 85186 053 3

Raven Arts Press receives financial assistance from The
Arts Council (an Chomhairle Ealaíon), Dublin, Ireland.

Cover design by Susanne Linde/Dermot Bolger.
Front cover photo by David Farrell, back photo by Podge
O'Farrell.
Printed in Ireland by Future Print, Baldoyle. Bound by Duffy
Bookbinding, Dublin.
Typeset in Ireland by The Carlow Nationalist.

CONTENTS

I

II

THE LAST OF DEEDS

ONE

We've all done it. Imagined our own funerals. The church is overflowing. There is unrestrained weeping. A woman dressed in black stands at the back of the crowd then steps forward to lay a wreath. The face is veiled but the hands are beautifully manicured, the nails long and red, cuticles stripped with orange stick and the skin so fine it is almost transparent so that the tips of the fingers are drops of milky water. There is some scandalised whispering and men eye their wives wishing it to be over, earth rustling like sheets on the lid of the coffin.

At least that's how I imagine it. Other people probably have their own way. When they buried Deeds I eyed the crowd expectantly. If anyone had deserved a beautiful stranger it was Deeds.

Not that I wasn't used to being in graveyards. There was the time they dug up the old graveyard in the middle of the town to build a new roundabout. Deeds, Jammy and me used to go down there at night when the workmen had left. There were graves exposed everywhere and the lids of the coffins were as thin as old parchment. In one corner they had just dug up bones because it had been a paupers graveyard and they buried the dead in a hinged deal coffin which could be used again and again.

The coffin was laid over the grave and the bottom opened so that the corpses of the poor tumbled into the earth with a wet slap.

Then again maybe they didn't make any noise at all because the corpses of the poor don't weigh anything. Maybe the gravediggers had to shovel earth into their faces so that they wouldn't float to the top again.

There was the ruin of a church in the graveyard as well with a union jack flying from the steeple because the dead must have some kind of politics. Binty said that some countries used to dig up the bones of soldiers from battlefields and export them for fertilizer. Millions of bones in the holds of ships and the noise that must have made, Binty said.

Here they took the bones away in sand lorries and dumped them down at the Banks.

The first couple of nights we just walked around looking at the graves and then one evening Deeds jumped into one and put his foot through the coffin lid. He came out of the grave with a skull in his hand. Then he started going round all the graves and getting the skulls. Some of them were so old that they fell apart in his hands like waterlogged bread. When he had enough he lined them up on the wall and took out his catapult which he had made from an old piece of aluminium and the tube from a bicycle tyre. The skulls on the wall were grinning at him and he was grinning back as he blasted them to dust and fragments with steel ball bearings.

"The living revenge themselves upon the dead," he said, and laughed.

You stand at the back of a funeral and wait for something to happen. You wait for the beautiful stranger because you know that in a few minutes the funeral will be over and men will come with shovels which will sound like torn silk when they bite into the earth and the earth will sound like sheets when it falls on the lid of the coffin and that will be the end.

On the outskirts of the town there is an avenue lined with trees. The legend is that there is a red woman who waits up the Avenue at night and that she has long strangling hands. Then you learn that there are no ghosts but that Cupids disco is beside the Avenue and the ground under the trees is littered with used condoms like worms after rain. And you learn that if you go up there on a Saturday night after Cupids the snap of buttons undone and the rattle of catches unfastened can be detected when the shifting and moistening of many bodies sounds like death.

The Avenue leads from Mill Street to the new estates of the Desmesne where you would think the houses are elegant if you saw them at night when the windows are lit and the smell of cooking is in the air. But during the day you can see the whitewash blacken and peel with salt carried in from the sea and how the dune grass encroaches on lawns and gardens. And if you look closely late at night you see videos flicker behind the curtains like light undressing itself.

There were plenty of stories about the people who lived in those houses. The Scout called them readers wives. You knew what he meant. They were like the women in the readers wives section of porn mags with a block of print over their faces like the stamp of a prison censor. In the background of those photographs you see the things you would find in any of those houses. The settee from the discount warehouse, the leather-bound books on pine shelves, the TV, the video. And out in front birth-stretched breasts lolling like tongues out of rubber bras and cunts like something you'd find on the dump. And the shops in town have racks full of porn mags so that you wonder where they all come from, all that pucker, glisten and gape. It might be your daughter or your sister. Someone's anyhow.

The river goes through the centre of the town past the warehouse where Deeds and Jammy had the loft and then it empties into the Harbour. Every week a big Polish boat comes in over the bar to moor beside the Plant. The boat stays for a day or two and sometimes you can hear the music that Sharon heard and then it will go out past the pier leaving half-slices of bread, bottles and pieces of wood coated with oil floating in corners of the Harbour.

If you stand on the pier wall where Deeds and Jammy painted their names you can see the concrete shelter on top of the Banks with the toilets at the back. There are still scorchmarks on the wall of the toilets where we lit fires. There is still a broken urinal flushing endlessly and the east wind carrying spray over the Harbour wall and through the empty doorframe of the shelter until your clothes acquired a saline odour, a deepwater smell.

TWO

He got the name Deeds at school when Boyle, the principal, got him by the throat and thrust his chalky, bald head into his face and hissed your misdeeds will be the death of me. Deeds had a round moon face with wire glasses that fitted his big head closely. He had hands the size of lunchboxes and his voice was soft like wings. When Jammy was listening to Deeds voice you could tell that he wanted to reach out and touch it as if it was a bird. Jammy loved pigeons and he helped Deeds build the loft and look after the birds. Jammy always had six inches of snot hanging from his sleeve and a chinful of pimples on the verge of bursting. Deeds hair was cropped close to his skull so that you could see blue scars through it but Jammy had long greasy hair that got caught around his face. One day at school a teacher used Jammy's hair to lift him off his feet with Jammy saying pleasesir, pleasesir very softly.

When his father was alive Jammy lived with him in an old council house near the Harbour. His father came home every night from the pub using both sides of the road. Jammy would lie awake in bed listening for his footsteps but the only thing he would hear was the scratch of tiny claws as rats chewed the house apart. Then one night Jammy's father fell into the Harbour on the way home. The scratch of tiny claws was the last thing he heard as crabs crossed the Harbour bottom to feed on the corpse.

They put the loft on top of the old warehouse on the river. They found the wood they needed on the banks of the river and covered it with scraps of paint, tar and cresosote. There was a run made of chicken wire at the front. Inside they kept bags of meal, pliers for ringing the pigeons legs, carrying baskets and ointments for toe rot and other diseases. And pigeons: blues, grays, fantails.

Deeds would take a pigeon in his cupped hands like water

12

to blow its breastfeathers apart or stroke them against the grain with his forefinger.

"Look at that," he would say, "if an angel was going to fly like a pigeon it would have to have a chest ten feet wide to get off the ground."

To safeguard the approach to the roof Deeds had come up with a system of ladders which would come away from the wall, holes in the roof disguised by loose tiles, gutters weakened so that if you put a foot wrong they would tilt and throw you into the river seventy or eighty feet below. Snakes and Ladders he called it.

He liked to sit with his legs over the edge of the roof watching pigeons fly up the river and the way they stayed close to the walls of the house on either side for protection. Sometimes Jammy would put them in baskets and they would take them out to a gray plantation of fir trees on the edge of town. Deeds would release the pigeons and watch them fly in a tight homing circle while Jammy hopped from foot to foot in case something happened to them.

It's hard to tell when things start. That's what Deeds used to say. Like one day you look up and see the settee and the pine shelves and the video and you want to know where it started and how far back you have to go. Maybe the first time you touched her and her inhalations became brief and quick. Or maybe you have to go further back than that.

We were down at the Harbour one day when Deeds said it about going to Cupids. It was the beginning of December when the streetlights come on in the estates before it is properly dark and the smoke of fires collects closer to the roofs. Women hurry when they are carrying the shopping to their cars. The rain comes in from the sea and the sea is gray. The orangemen stop marching through the town so that you don't hear the sound of their preachers talking through public address systems which has sounded like a radio in another room all Summer.

Deeds had found a tin of paint behind the Plant. We took it up to the pier and Deeds painted his name on the pier wall. He took his time, using big letters you could see all over the Harbour. When he finished Jammy had to have his name done as well.

Jammy was pleased with it. He started to kick the empty

paint tin along the pier. There were threads of paint coming out of it and wrapping themselves around his shins.

"You're not half-wise Jammy," Deeds said. Jammy dribbled the tin to the edge of the dock and kicked it out over the water.

"Goal," he shouted, "one-nil."

The tin filled up and sank. Deeds lit a cigarette and leaned against the pier wall.

"We're going to Cupids tomorrow night," he said.

"What for?" Jammy asked.

"I'm going to get my hole."

"Who with?"

"Never you mind, you chicken or something?"

Jammy tried to say something but couldn't. When he got nervous he had a speech defect where his tongue came to the edge of his lips and stayed there like some fat, shiny parasite. In the end he just shook his head.

"Anne-Marie Hicks," Deeds said. We saw her every day in The Submarine Cafe.

The Submarine had yellow lace curtains hard as wax because of the grease in the air. The tables had blue plastic on top. There was a pool table in the back and a poker machine. The stainless steel urn streamed, fogging the windows. Greasespots separated and merged on the surface of the tea and you could make a tea last for the afternoon while the fish fryer crackled and drenched the air around you.

During the day she was a waitress at The Submarine. At night she was in Cupids. If she wasn't there she was hanging round the Harbour and sometimes one of the workers from the Plant would take her behind the coastguard station and return with his heart frozen and his clothes impregnated with the smell of chip fat and salt cunt.

She had a small mouth and huge breasts, the blue and white checked nylon of her apron rustling as she walked among the tables. Deeds swore that if you listened you could hear the sound of sex as well like the dull lapping of animals drinking.

We left the Submarine and went to the loft. When we got there we sat on the edge of the roof. You could see all of Mill Street and right down the Harbour road as far as the Harbour. The streets were wet and you could see the wet blackness of the rooftiles on buildings. There were hardly any people about. Deeds took a Frenchie out of his pocket and split the foil with his thumb. He unrolled it and blew it up like a balloon. Then he tied a knot in the end and let it go. He did the same with another. We sat on the roof and watched them go down over the river like pink, silk parachutes, weaving when the wind brushed them.

THREE

Binty said that the Harbour used to be a big fishing port until the war when a U-boat surfaced in the middle of the fleet. It was black with rust on the hatches, he said, as if he had been there. It had a big gun at the front, and when it submerged, fuming with compressed air escaping from valves, there were just jellyfish of oil and splintered planks where the fishing boats used to be.

Binty told Jammy that the U-boat was still out there. Half a century of polishing torpedoes and replacing detonators in cramped and foetid quarters. Surfacing at night for air or from habit. You hear stories of Japanese soldiers who have survived in the jungle for decades after the war, a picture of the emperor in their foxholes, while mildew claimed their uniforms and the bark of flying foxes claimed their minds. Jammy didn't know what to believe.

Binty lived with Minnie Toal in the shelter at the top of the Banks. The Banks were brick-coloured cliffs overlooking the shingle beach beside the Harbour. The shelter was just a concrete shed with benches in it and broken toilets at the back. Binty said it was put there so that people coming out for walks could sit in it. But nobody ever came for a walk on the Banks and there were grass clippings, old bottles and builders rubble piled at the foot of the cliffs.

We did our drinking at the Banks. Most of the time we drank vodka. You put the bottle to your mouth, tilted it back and bolted vodka. At first it would be cold like shutting your teeth on bone or china but it would be warm and bitter after that, sitting outside the shelter with a fire or perched up on the roof feeling like you could reach up and touch the big, glass lip of the moon above you.

There was a car park on the Esplanade behind the Banks and cars with couples in them would park there at night. The cars would start creaking and moving after a while. Sometimes there would be fifteen or twenty cars in different

16

parts of the car park, all moving with hollow noises. Deeds would say that the town was breeding and go over to bang on the window of a car or rip the boot into the side of it and the movement would stop. They might drive off after that, but usually the movement would start again, slowly at first.

The next night we met at the Banks about eight o'clock. Jammy went to the off-licence and Deeds lit a fire against the wall of the toilets. By the time Jammy came back the fire had caught and the sandy area around the toilets began to look like some kind of desert with Deeds sitting in the middle of it saying that he was the sheik, the sheik of Araby, and laughing to himself.

"Hold the bus," Jammy said after a while, "Minnie's on the warpath."

I looked around and saw her coming out of the shelter. She had red eyes and gray hair with pink bald patches in it. She had a big nose like a vegetable covered in broken veins and blackheads. When she walked her bony pelvis stuck out from under her skirt. But it was her stomach that made you stop and look, the way it rested on the knobs of her pelvis like an egg held between the tips of two fingers.

"Roll over in the bed", Deeds said, when he saw her rushing towards the fire. But Jammy didn't need to be told. She made him nervous. When Minnie and Binty were in the shelters drinking bottles of Buckfast Tonic Wine or VP sherry, Minnie would complain about her kidneys and then she'd go outside the shelter and squat. When she got up there would be a small pool of old woman's piss on the ground. Jammy couldn't get over it. Every time she did it he'd meet your eye in the darkness.

Minnie warmed her hands at the fire without looking at any of us. Deeds just shrugged and kept on drinking. Jammy moved round to the other side of the fire. When I looked up again I saw Binty standing just outside the firelight, his eyes squinting at us along the length of his big nose as if it was a brass telescope.

"How's Binty?" Deeds asked.

"Not the worst," Binty said, moving closer to the fire.

"Youse must have been having a wee bit of a court up in the shelter there," Deeds said.

"Did you slip her one?" Jammy asked.

"Pups," Minnie said, "I'd warm your arses so I would." She got up from the fire and walked away. Then she sat down in the sand and started to run handfuls of it through her fingers.

"Don't mind her," Binty said, "she's not well in herself these days."

"You don't fool us," Deeds said.

"We know what you were up to," Jammy said. Binty just shook his head and sat down beside Deeds. Deeds passed him the bottle.

We sat there for a few hours. When the vodka was finished Binty went to the shelter and brought back a bottle of Buckfast. Jammy collected more wood from the beach and put it on the fire. There must have been tar on some of the wood because through the sweet smell of the driftwood there was the black, rubber smell of tar burning.

Binty told us how the Glennons used to own a mill just outside the town. He said there was a canal which they used to take cargo from the mill. Oceangoing ships went up the canal and it looked as if they were sailing on dry land in some mystical way. The workers went out to the mill by tram and in the evenings Binty stood at the bottom of the street where the tramlines ended, selling silk stockings to the millgirls when they came off the trams, letting them run the material through their wishing fingers, pitted and black from needles and chemicals.

But there was no sign of a mill or a canal now if they ever existed. Just the fire on the rim of Deeds glasses and Binty's watchful talk about silk as smooth as glass that wouldn't run, how women loved it next to the skin and Deeds putting in something about how silkworms had eleven brains and Binty explaining how they boiled the worms to get the silk from them.

The glamour of thousands of tiny mouths chewing leaves then silenced into pulpy corpses. I couldn't see it. All I could hear was Minnie's mumbling.

"The town's rotten, rotten drink, rotten men, rotten money."

In the end Deeds stood up.

"Are you right," he said, "the old biddy's yap is getting on my nerves."

We crossed the Esplanade and walked up the Harbour road until we reached Mill Street where we turned right. There was me, Deeds and Jammy and we were all wearing white tartan scarves which was Deeds idea.

There were cars lined up along the kerb on either side of Mill Street. I don't know what it is about this town, the way they sit in cars on a Friday or Saturday night. There could be three or four people in each car or there could be none. Every so often a match strikes to light a cigarette and you can see that area of shadow between the lips and the eyes. Later perhaps a hand crosses between the seats, the shadows meet. There is a catch in the breath under the shadows.

That's not all. When it gets late they start to drive around the town. They all seem to pull away from the kerb at the same time so maybe the striking of matches is some kind of language. I don't know.

They drive slowly down Mill Street, slowly down the Harbour road. One after another they circle the Harbour and come back up the Harbour road again, taking turns to pull off into the Esplanade car park. Sometimes they keep it up all night, those darkened cargoes wheeling on some interior axis you know nothing about.

Cupids is at the end of Mill Street, opposite the Avenue. It used to be a cinema and there is still the white, plastic sign over the door where they displayed the name of the film. But that has a big, red Cupid on it now. After it was a cinema it was a woodstore before they turned it into a disco and if you looked inside it during the day it looked monochrome and smelled of sap.

But that night it was hot inside, the air inhabited all the way up to the roof. You get a look at a face turned in the light, or a breast or a leg. Before long you can't recognise anybody. Places like that make you think of fires and bodies piled at the exit.

I drank a half-bottle with Deeds on the edge of the dancefloor. Jammy looked sick. He sat against the wall with his head in his hands.

Deeds got up to dance with Anne-Marie. After a while I saw that he had his arms around her and that they were moving very slowly. As I watched his hand dropped to where the ultra-violet light made her panties show white through her trousers.

Jammy got up and walked towards the toilets. I watched him go so that I didn't see the girl until she was standing in front of me. She was wearing wranglers and a white blouse with no sleeves. Her hair was cropped and even in that light you could see her skin was fine so that it looked as if there were blue shadows under it. When I danced with her I saw a union jack tattooed on her left arm above the elbow. She didn't look at me when she danced but then I felt her breath on my ear and her words like some distant, incomprehensible radio station when you recognise just one word and before I had a chance to answer Deeds was beside me telling me that Jammy had got a hiding in the bogs.

There were cubicles along one wall of the toilets and urinals on the other. There were sinks beside the urinals with specked mirrors above them. The light came from two bulbs. The reflection from the smeared blue tiles and the white porcelain hurt your eyes.

Deeds had found Jammy lying under the sinks. The floor around him was covered with wet scraps of paper towel from the plastic bin. There were red marks on his face and some blood. When we lifted him to his feet his head yawned back and forward. Then he put his forehead against the wall and started to throw up, the vomit making a loose sound on the floor.

We took Jammy out of the toilets and got him as far as the hallway behind the main door. Anne-Marie was there. She wet a tissue, making a squirting sound with her lips then she used it to clean Jammy's face. We started to move towards the exit. There was a crowd of Prods around the door. One of them stepped forward as we were going out. His name was Glennon. He was tall with a big spade-shaped head.

"Got the message?" he said.

"What fucking message?" Deeds said.

Glennon nodded at Jammy. I kept my eyes on the black and white tiles on the floor. I was ready. Deeds stopped walking and faced Glennon. Before either of them could move the girl with the cropped hair stepped in between them, putting her arm around Glennon's waist and made him turn away.

"Your sort aren't welcome here, that's the fucking

message," Glennon said as we pushed through the doors. I looked at Deeds. Glennon's father owned most of the town and there wasn't much you could do about him but I knew Deeds would have different ideas. That came later.

I heard the door swing open behind me. It was the girl with the cropped hair. She looked at Jammy and then she looked at the rest of us.

"I hope you're proud of yourselves," she said, "people are only trying to enjoy themselves and the likes of you only want to spoil it."

"We didn't start anything," Deeds said.

" You think you're smart," she said, "you just go looking for trouble."

Deeds didn't say anything. He started to walk off down Mill Street holding Jammy by the arm. Ann-Marie took the other arm. I watched them go. Then I turned around to look at her again. I had been right the first time. The pupils of her eyes were almost black, like beads of hot tar.

"What do you want?" she said.

"Nothing."

"Well what are you hanging around here for?"

"Nothing."

"Nothing," she said, "Mr Nothing". She walked to the door and cupped her hands to look through the mesh of the reinforced glass. Then she came back.

"Alright," she said, "come on if you're coming."

She was quiet until we reached the entrance to the Avenue. She took my arm there.

"What's your name?" I asked.

"Sharon, Shazz the Razz". She laughed, moving closer and starting to talk. I knew why she wanted to talk. The Avenue after Cupids was like a field hospital at night. Couples behind each tree, breathing in the dark, sometimes a voice, patients talking in their sleep out of drugged pain.

She worked in the Plant. Mostly filleting dead fish that came in frozen slabs from the big Polish boats, handbags of guts looted and dumped. Sometimes there would be a cargo of prawns to be shelled that would crackle and stab the hands and leave them bleeding.

Half the girls in the town worked at the Plant, their soft, tissue hats the only virtue in the wet and cold civilisation of

21

fish.

Then she stopped talking and pushed me back against a tree, kissing me so hard that our teeth met and the feeling of it went right back into my skull.

"I always wanted somebody like you," she said. I was surprised.

When I pulled her down to the ground she came as if she had no weight but she twisted at the last moment so that I was on my back and she was on top of me. I felt her hands on my face, locating it in the dark. I put my hand on her breast. Through her blouse I could feel the jagged fringe of lace on her bra. I moved my hand down where it was softer. She put her hand on my neck. I rotated her nipple with my thumb. When I couldn't breathe any more I put my other hand to her face and found the loop of her earring in the soft, blue place under the line of her jaw. I kept pressure on it until I thought her ear would tear. Her mouth came down to meet mine then and I could breathe again.

When it was over she sat with her back to a tree, legs drawn up to her buttocks. I gave her a cigarette and we smoked.

"You're a Taig," she said. I didn't say anything. I knew she was a Prod the first time I saw her.

"They'll kill me," she said, "I don't care." Through the trees I thought I could see the lights of cars on the Harbour road. I heard the noise of engines starting as if her words had been the signal.

FOUR

Deeds nudged soft blue chalk onto the tip of the cue and stood back from the table.

"She's as black as your boot," he said, putting his hand flat on the rubbed, green felt of the table, the cue running between the knuckles of his thumb and forefinger.

"The da's a reserve cop. The whole family's in it, lock, stock and barrel. UDR, RUC, you name it."

"Prods," Jammy said.

"So what," I said, "play the ball."

"No skin off my nose," Deeds said.

"Did you get the tit," Jammy said. He was standing in the corner with his hands padding the big buttons of the poker machine.

"You'll get another split lip if you don't mind yourself," Deeds said.

A yellow went down in the middle pocket but the slope of the table carried the white ball into the bottom corner. I took the cue.

"Don't worry about it," I said.

"Stop the lights," Jammy said, "it's the Scout."

We looked into the main part of the cafe. You could see his face against the window, his hand scraping a ragged seam in the streaked dirt on the outside of the glass.

"Shite," Deeds said, "he's coming in."

I had my back to the door when he came in but I knew who it was. It was the same every time. He was about the town all hours of the day and night. You never knew where he would be next but every time you passed him in the dark you wondered if you'd dreamed that sick feeling that left you sweating like old cheese.

When I looked again he was standing in the doorway of the poolroom, one hand in his pocket, the other paralysed in a black leather glove and tapping his trouser leg.

They said he didn't sleep and you could believe it. If you lived in this town you carried those eyes with you. One good eye looking through you and the other one bulging from the socket, tilted and useless. No matter how tightly you drew the curtains you couldn't keep those eyes out. At night he'd be watching up the Avenue or down behind the coastguard station. In the morning you saw him in the Desmesne maybe, watching women's clothes on the washing-lines, giggling at the way they dived and swooped like turtles on the Gulf Stream and rubbing himself through the lining of his pocket until a stain the shape and colour of a copper coin appeared on the front of his trousers.

"My wee angels," he said, looking at us. I watched his mouth. It looked as if his lips were stuck together with all sorts of things. Lint, grease, feathers. He had a sick mouth.

"I hear young Deeds got the leg over the Hicks girl last night. That's a man's work so that is. There's not many come away scot free from that. There's a quare lonely place up inside that one. I'd mind she doesn't trap you. I seen that too."

"Seen what?" Jammy asked.

"I seen it happen. Are you trying to take a hand out of me young Jammy because if you are I'm fit for you."

Jammy drew back, all eyes, and shook his head. The Scout stared at him.

"Hold your horses," he said, "I won't eat you yet. I'm telling you what I seen. I seen your baldy master Boyle up to the hilt one night in the back of the car and she got a hold of him and wouldn't let go. The fanny muscles lock up. Fit to be tied so he was with her all sweetness and her spit running down his chops.

"Your misdeeds will be the death of me," Jammy said and giggled.

All the time the Scout was talking his gloved hand plucked at his trousers, raising the material in tufts.

"I'll say nothing about you," he said, looking at me. I held his eye, looking into its dark pupil, cupped in a bowl of white that was streaked with estuaries of veins.

"Mad in the head," Deeds said.

"One eye looking at you and the other looking for you," Jammy said.

I looked again and saw the Scout's back as the door closed behind him.

"Are you going to stand there all day," Deeds said, "or are you going to take that shot?"

Afterwards we went to the loft to feed the birds. To get to it you had to go down behind the houses on the Harbour road and cross the river, jumping from stone to stone. There was a gap in the wall between the warehouse and the water and you could climb through. There was old machinery in the yard in front of the warehouse. Winches and engines soldered together with rust. Going up the ladder you could see into the big empty windows. The air coming out of them smelt of rotting sacks and bonemeal even though it was a long time since they kept anything in there and all the floors had fallen through so that it was hollow and brown like a tooth.

Binty said that Albert Glennon owned the warehouse and that it had belonged to the Mill.

When we got to the roof Deeds took one pigeon in his cupped hands as if it was water and threw it up into the air so that you thought he had spilled it until you heard the clap of wings on air like soft valves opening and shutting.

"We're going to race them," Deeds said, "me and Jammy."

He went back into the loft. I sat on the edge of the roof. There was smoke over the roofs of the town and mist on the river. Down the street I saw Binty come out of the off-licence and sit in a doorway, looking across the street as if dreams of millgirls were walking on the opposite pavement, passing into invisibility. It was quiet and I heard sparrows in the evening between the black, geometric telephone wires.

FIVE

I saw a film star on TV once who said that she tried to walk as if she was carrying a small coin between her buttocks. I thought about that when I saw Sharon coming up the Harbour road wearing flat shoes and a white acrylic skirt with fish blood on it and walking as if she was wearing high heels and carrying a coin between her buttocks or something moister and more private like a pigeon's egg between her thighs.

I knew that her shift ended at five so I had waited at the top of the Harbour road until the horn went at the Plant. Even if I had known what Deeds was planning for the next day I would still have waited.

All the girls leaving the factory had the same white, acrylic skirts and tissue hats but some of them were wearing jackets or cardigans over their uniforms. They left the Plant in groups which thinned out as they got towards the top of the hill. She was walking on her own. She didn't stop walking when she saw me. I took her arm.

"What do you want?"

"Nothing."

"You're not wise," she said and smiled. "Look," she said quickly, "you know our park?" I nodded.

"Wait on the corner of it around eleven tonight. Mind nobody sees you."

"Shazz the Razz," I said.

"That's right," she said, and leaned towards me, putting her mouth next to my cheek. The bite left two tiny footprints in the skin that wouldn't have faded completely by the time the whole thing was over. I watched her walk away, the wind pushing her skirt against the back of her knees and the dark creases there.

There were streetlights everywhere in the Desmesne. Orange lozenges floating in the damp air. I stepped back into

26

the doorway of a garage and wondered which house was Sharon's. They all had the same roofs with red asbestos tiles and big windows blank with curtains or with light curling round the slats of venetian blinds.

She came around the back of the house opposite me and stood beside me in the doorway, not touching. I remembered the ultra-violet light in Cupids, Deeds hand placed on Ann-Marie's buttocks and the white of her panties shining through. I wondered how the light had escaped picking out the white bones on Sharon's face, the unimaginable lingerie of death.

She led me around the back of the houses where I followed her over a wall made of breezeblocks and into a back garden. There was a washing-line in the garden, a tricycle and a shrunken, plastic football. There was a bucket of cinders at the back door to avoid. A bedroom window was open and we climbed in through it.

And when we were in the room there was a mirror, a dressing table with bottles, the smell of her. I picked up a bottle and smelled it. She took a nightdress from beneath a pillow and undressed under it.

She got into bed: I lifted the nightdress over her breasts and smelled her private warmth. When I tried to pull it over her head she stopped me. Her nipples were hard, squeezed into pellets and she got on top of me. After that we didn't kiss. I could feel her head against my cheek and her lips moving when she spoke her brief language into the pillow.

I climbed out of the window into a gray light which was mist by the time I reached the Banks.

The tide was out, exposing old cars and rusting tangles of steel cable. Further out the seabed must have been covered in rotting and leaking pieces of metal. Old exhausts, winches, bones, television sets. You could see the long concrete outline of the sewer outlet. If you walked to the end of it at low tide you could see where the water turned red with the effluent from McConville's slaughter yard. Sometimes plastic tampon holders came out of the end of the pipe in flocks, like birds paddling out to sea on tiny, pink feet.

You could nearly believe there was a submarine out there, trapped under the weight of blood and iron. I lit a cigarette. My eyes felt gritty, my balls were a warm sore parcel. Binty came out of the shelter stretching, and stood beside me.

"If this was Australia," he said after a while, "that would be a sunset out there."

Minnie came out of the shelter after him. She stood on the other side.

"Like a great big bloody egg," she said.

"What is?"

"The sun," she said, pointing through the mist.

SIX

That afternoon I met Deeds and Jammy in The Submarine. It was Saturday and there were more people than usual in the cafe. When I shut my eyes voices disappeared into exhausted static, a slab of cod in hot fat like hair burning, the hot spout of the coffee machine muzzled in cold milk.

Anne-Marie was carrying plates of half-eaten chips and ketchup back to the kitchen.

We took a table in the corner. Jammy spillled salt onto the table and traced his name in it. Deeds sat with his chair tilted onto its back legs, picking threads from the cuff of his jacket with one hand while the other cupped a cigarette and smoked it into a tight ducks arse. Deeds had told me about the ambush so I wasn't surprised when I saw JB and Haresy come in through the door and look around for us.

Haresy was called that because of his face, but it wasn't a hare lip. He had been hit with a bottle. The split lip was badly stitched and the nose was knocked sideways.

They came from the Chalk City which was an old housing estate out beyond Cupids. The houses were white going gray with brickwork showing in places where the plaster had collapsed. The thin hedges between the houses were broken and trampled and the roadway was blocked by old cars, sumps and exhausts hanging out. There was a shop with heavy wire mesh over its windows and a sheet of metal on the door. At night it was dark in the Chalk City because the bulbs of the street lights had been broken and their lead cables stripped.

You imagined that Haresy gnawed his way out of the Chalk City every so often with his torn lips hanging round his yellow teeth and JB came with him like a ghost because even though he was so big he was smooth-skinned and silent so that you hardly knew he was there.

Haresy and JB ordered tea. When they finished it we walked to the top of the Harbour road. Deeds stood in a doorway and the rest of us crouched behind a wall. We waited for a long time. I remember JB turning to me and remarking how cold it was.

After another length of time we heard Deeds whistle. It was the signal and the rest of them turned to look at me. I looked down and saw a beetle climbing over a leaf. Before I had finished the beetle came out from underneath. I flipped the leaf again and climbed the wall with the rest of them behind me.

It worked so that Glennon was trapped half-way between Deeds, who had stepped out from behind the doorway, and the rest of us. Glennon looked at Deeds then looked back at the rest of us and stopped walking. He took his hands out of his pockets and left them swinging by his sides, Deeds walked right up to him and hesitated, wanting Glennon to strike first, but he didn't so Deeds turned sideways to him, swivelled on one foot and kicked him hard in the crotch with the other. Glennon took two steps backwards, cradling his balls but not saying anything. Then Deeds swung his fist.

It was a quiet Winter's day going on towards evening. Everything was slate-gray and very still. There was the sound that an apple makes when you pull the two halves apart. Glennon went down with blood on his mouth.

It was counterfeit and we all knew it. I started to see faces, photographs, men behind barbed wire, a woman with a child on her hip and flies on her eyes, a man watching a plume of smoke rising from hills that weren't far enough away. Mortals. I wanted to know what we were doing there.

Deeds just stood looking at the body on the ground as if it were a crack that had opened in the pavement. Then he turned and walked past us as if we were invisible.

Afterwards Deeds said that he felt as if he had suddenly lost touch with everything. Not that anything had changed but that he himself had become unreal, like a ghost. I looked at him and laughed but he didn't.

We went back to the Submarine but nobody had anything much to say. Deeds and Jammy went to the loft and the others drifted home. I sat in The Submarine until it closed. Then I walked down the Harbour road to the Banks. The sea was churning at the base of the cliffs so that it looked like the washed-out remains of a fire. I saw the Scout coming but I stayed where I was, watching him, the way he moved, stepping out with one foot and lifting the other side of his body with a kind of shrug to get the stiff leg forward.

I thought he hadn't seen me until he stopped, the leather glove rattling against his leg with a sound like black sticks breaking. Then he was beside me, rocking backwards and forwards on his heels so that you felt somehow he was still walking through streets and estates at night and you wanted to tell people to turn out the light before they undressed and then to lie in bed side by side without moving or even breathing but they don't and you're watching and hearing all the small sad cries of fear and perhaps of death.

Put four walls around it, The Scout said, moving his good hand so that it took in the whole town, and a roof over it and you'd have the biggest whorehouse in the world.

Then he was gone again. I looked at the town. He might have been right but the way I saw it at that moment the whole town might have gone missing so that there was nothing between the streetlights.

I started back up the Harbour road. At one place the road was narrow where the red brick houses backed onto the river. The houses had no hallway between the street and the living-room so that when I looked in through one open door I saw a television set in the corner. It must have been showing the news because there were pictures of soldiers with tanks on sunlit streets that ran between small, white houses and there were children standing around so that you wondered if somewhere off those dusty streets there were trees with real oranges on them.

SEVEN

But then Deeds would say that there were always wars and things going on all over the world. You just had to get used to it. Like you'd be sitting in The Submarine and there'd be a famine in Africa. No matter what you're doing it's happening everywhere. Two people are getting in or out of bed with each other, humping and grunting. Noises you can't drown out. In beds, cars, cinemas, pavements even, all those different languages. And when you reach over to flick your cigarette into the ashtray or something like that there are women screaming giving birth and people dying in rooms as the curtains glide together until they're shut, with light and noise in the street outside, and no one has the strength to open their mouths to let out the sound of their breathing.

A few weeks after the fight with Glennon I was down at the Banks. Deeds was with Anne-Marie and there was no sign of Jammy except for the embers of a fire which had been lit earlier against the wall of the toilets. Binty sat on a piece of timber at one side of the fire and I sat at the other side. He was telling me how he had seen a dogfight over the Harbour once. It was a Sunday and people used to walk at the Harbour on a Sunday afternoon. The two planes were up there for a long time. Then one spouted a trail of black smoke and turned its nose towards the sea. They all saw the parachute open and drift towards the shingle beach below the Banks. The wind pulled the dead pilot over the shingle and his heels made a clicking noise on the stones.

"Hundreds of yards of pure silk," Binty said, "and your man in the middle of it."

I heard a scuffle in the sand outside the firelight and I looked up. Sharon was standing there, breathing hard. Binty got to his feet and offered her the piece of timber but she shook her head without looking at him.

"Fancy a walk around the Harbour?" she asked me. I got

up from the fire. Binty was looking straight at her.

"You'll freeze without a jacket," he said, "stay by the fire." She was wearing the same blouse as she had been wearing in Cupids. She shook her head again. I took my jacket off and she put it around her shoulders. Binty put his hand on my arm.

"Mind yourselves," he said quietly.

I didn't say anything immediately. We walked quickly along the Banks towards the Harbour and came out behind the coastguard station where you could see the glow of radar screens behind the windows and a man's head, detecting lost objects circulating in the dark.

"What's eating you?" I asked.

"Nothing," she said.

"Where were you going with no coat?" I asked.

"Nowhere," she said.

"Nowhere," I said, "Mrs Nowhere."

"I'm not in the mood," she said, breaking away from me and sliding down the slope beside the coastguard station. I followed her, down the slope and through the tangle of old cable and broken fishboxes at the bottom. She went along the back of the Plant. There was a brightly lit compound there, with lorry trailers parked in rows, the refrigerator units at the back of the trailers making a low sound that you could hear from a distance.

She went around the edge of the compound and came out on the other side at a place where the fence was in shadow. I saw her pull her skirt up to her waist to climb the green spiked fence. She didn't wait on the other side. I got over quickly and went after her, crossing a small patch of grass and then onto a concrete path which was slippery where frost spilled like the cold nitrates in the heart of stone. She stopped at a low concrete building attached to one side of the Plant. There were small windows at shoulder height. One of them was broken. She slipped her hand through the broken pane to undo the catch then she pulled herself onto the sill and wriggled through. As I followed her through the window I heard her say upsadaisy from inside and giggle. On the other side the floor was wet so that your feet mewed on it when you walked. It was dark but there was a light coming from a doorway so that you could see the white bird shapes of urinals.

33

She called me from the door, softly, like someone keeping a secret. She took my hand and we went out onto a corridor which was like a school corridor with doors opening off it. There were globe lights hanging from the ceiling. It felt hollow walking along there with those lights crawling on the ceiling like big moths.

Outside, on the Banks, it couldn't have taken very long, kicking Binty on the ground until his loose and broken bones started to slick around under his skin. You imagine that nothing was said, that both of them were intent, Binty intent and holding his breath until a solid kick that forced the others breath out forced Binty's breath out from between his lips as well, the two of them making a brief language that could not be heard.

The corridor led to the section of the Plant where the filleting was done. There was a time clock on the wall inside the door of the filleting section with overalls hanging on pegs beside it. The light came from fluorescent strips attached to the roof girders. I saw the place where she worked. There was a slab of wood in front of a conveyor belt with a stand beside it. There were more slabs and stands on either side of the conveyor belt.

You put a box of fish on the stand, she said. You put a fish on the slab and lifted the knife with a blade which had been sharpened so often that it had become thin and almost transparent towards the edge. The swim bladder stomach, lungs and all the other organs come out easily. Then you fold the two sides of the fish outwards like wings and put it on the conveyor belt.

I heard a siren and it was about that time that Jammy had come back to the Banks and had seen the disturbed earth at the edge of the cliff and Binty face down in the builders rubble, grass clippings and old bottles at the bottom of the cliff and had run to the coastguard station to phone, hardly able to get the words out.

Sharon was standing in front of the slab with the knife in her hand, looking down at the blade.

"Do you know what I'd do if you ever two-timed me," she said, "I'd cut your balls off."

I walked across the wet floor and put my hands on her breasts from behind. She put the knife down and turned to

34

face me. We were like that for a while, struggling, then she pushed me away.

"I need to pee," she said.

When they were lifting Binty out of the ambulance at the hospital we walked along the corridor with the moth lights back to the toilets. Sharon pushed a cubicle door open with her foot.

"Don't look," she said. I stood in the darkness while she stripped and squatted in a single movement. After a pause the rainy whistle of her urine sounded in the bowl while deft nurses fingers undid Binty's buttons. He was hard to handle, slippery, with bones hinged lightly in unexpected places so they started to cut through his shirt and trousers with big shears because even though he was dead they had to look, the shears rustling and even the nurses growing silent as if they expected to find wings neatly folded over the shoulderblades when in fact they saw an old man's body which is whiter than any silk which is worn next to the skin.

I listened to the sound of water for a long time until her bowels halted with a fledgling rustle when I heard footsteps on the corridor outside.

I looked at Sharon. Her eyes were closed and her lips were apart.

"Heaven," she said softly, "heaven."

EIGHT

It rained for a day and a night. The funeral took place in the rain so that Minnie's veil was stuck to her face and the yellow clay of the grave looked slick and waxy. I don't know where she got the veil. It was just a scrap of lace pinned to the front of her hair.

Everyone said it was an accident. They stood with umbrellas in the new graveyard outside the town saying it was an accident while flowers in plastic domes pushed up through the coloured stone chippings on the graves like transparent, dead foreheads.

Minnie was standing behind us at the graveside. Deeds whispered that she smelt like a brewery and Jammy started to laugh. They began to lower the coffin into the grave but just before it touched the bottom I saw soil starting to peel off the sides of the grave and then the sides collapsed and water started to pour in scattering fist-sized lumps of the yellow clay on the lid of the coffin. Nothing happened for a moment but you could see that the grave was filling with water and then the coffin began to rise again, floating on the water and bumping gently.

The water poured into the grave. It looked as if it was never going to stop and the coffin would float over the lip of the grave, out of the graveyard, past Cupids and the Avenue and the warehouses and the Plant, through the Harbour mouth and into the open sea.

In the end they had to lift the coffin out of the grave again and bring in a diesel pump to drain it. The pump could be heard late into the night and when it stopped there was the sound of shovels.

After the funeral we went back to The Submarine. Haresy was in the poolroom with a basket that Jammy had given him to look after during the funeral. Jammy opened the basket. There was a sick pigeon in it, lying on the floor with

36

its legs curled up. Its eyes were dull and soupy. It didn't move much except for every so often when it would put its beak down into its breastfeathers as if it was going to preen itself but the beak would just go into the feathers and stick there without moving. Jammy tried to give it some bread but it wouldn't take it.

Anne-Marie came into the room to wipe tables.

"I'd ride the arse off that," Haresy said so that she could hear, but she didn't say anything or even look at him.

"Watch," Deeds said. He went over to her and backed her against the wall, putting his hand on her cunt through the nylon apron. She didn't try to push him away. Her hands were hovering at the level of his shoulders like pink amputated nubs. I looked into her eyes and there was nothing there. Jammy and Haresy laughed.

"No flies on our Deeds," Jammy said. Deeds tried to kiss her but she turned her head away. The woman who owned the cafe came into the room and saw what was happening.

"Quit your codding around," she said, pointing at Deeds, "one of these days you'll go too far son." Deeds dropped his hands and Anne-Marie began to wipe tables as if nothing had happened.

"Fuck this," he said, "I'm going to the Banks."

It was the first time any of us had been back since Binty's death. There was yellow incident tape around the broken piece of bank and a police landrover on the Esplanade with its engine running.

You never looked directly at those landrovers. You knew there was somebody behind those narrow, bulletproof windows watching you like everything else in the town. You imagined the metal and loneliness of the interior and what it would be like if they got you inside one.

Jammy pointed at the spot where the body had been lying at the bottom of the cliff.

"Silly old bastard," Haresy said.

"The worms have him now," Deeds said, "making silk while the sun shines."

I was about to say something then. About the voices I heard that night in the factory. Sharon and me in the dark, not breathing, one voice inaudible and the other a man's voice saying how he'd fix it if the other would just keep his mouth shut and who's to say that it wasn't what it looked like anyway but that he could pull strings and they knew better than to cross him in this town when it came down to it.

But Deeds had crossed the path to the shelter and I saw him motion to me to come and look. I went over and put my head inside the door. Minnie was sitting on one of the benches. She had a bottle in her hand and her cardigan had ridden up, exposing her stomach. Jammy nudged me when he saw that brown, tight thing sitting in her lap like a big nut. She was talking to herself as if there was nobody there.

"Rotten hole, rotten fucking hole, all them men hanging about for a bit of a touch, that's all they want, you'd think they were something, Binty Quinn yapping on about how silk stockings would become your smooth calves, become your smooth calves my arse, all he's looking for is a wee grope when he feels like it same as the rest of them."

But she knew that we were there because she turned and pulled the cardigan further up.

"Go on, have a touch," she said, "that's what youse all want. Touch the baby."

She was laughing now. Jammy was looking at her belly with the blind navel and the thick, unborn knots in it and he looked as if he was about to give her a dig to make her stop.

"Youse are afraid," she said, jeering. Suddenly Deeds got down beside her and put his big hand against her belly. His hand was cupped as if for listening. Minnie shut her eyes. She just lay there with her mouth open until Deeds got up and walked away.

"Like magic," Deeds said quietly and when I looked back Minnie was crying like any ordinary old woman.

"That's some gut she has on her," Haresy said outside, "she was up the chute and she tried to hoke the baby out with a coathanger and she blew up like a balloon. So they say anyhow."

"You wouldn't want to believe everything you hear," Deeds said.

We walked back towards the town to go to the off-licence. Jammy brought the pigeon back to the loft and we waited for him on the bridge which crossed the river at Mill Street.

We sat on the parapet and watched gulls fighting over fish heads which were dumped at the Plant and carried upstream by the tide. The gulls took the eyes so that all you could see was bleak sockets looking up.

"That child of Minnie's," Haresy said, "the one she got rid of, you'd wonder who the da was."

"Never mind," Deeds said, "everybody's got their secrets."

I watched the river going past and for some reason I thought of the people who shut their eyes when they saw the cattle trucks going past on their way to concentration camps even though they knew those miles of rail would go on jolting through their childrens' heads.

NINE

Down at the Banks I watched the rain make black marks in the sand. There was nothing else to do. Haresy had gone home when the drink was finished. Jammy sat with his back to the toilet wall with threads of hair being blown across his open mouth. Deeds lay on the ground with a bottle between his knees. The fire smoked and the wind sometimes blew the smoke back towards us.

Other nights we would have been listening to stories that might or might not have been true, half-remembered plots of boats that sailed on dry land, airmen from old wars, fine ankles and calves almost invisible under the gauze of silk and time.

I looked up when I heard the crack of broken glass against the wall. Deeds hand was empty and Jammy was staring at him.

"What did you do that for? "Jammy said.

"What's it to you anyway?" Deeds said. He got to his feet. The firelight made bright spools in the lens of his glasses. He aimed a kick at Jammy's head but his foot slipped in the sand and he landed on his back. He didn't move until Jammy came over and lifted him onto his feet.

They walked off across the Esplanade. Jammy supported Deeds. I could see Jammy was talking to him the way he made kissing noises when he handled a pigeon.

I had some cigarettes left and I smoked one sitting by the fire. The rain became heavier, with sleet mixed in it. The sound of the waves on the shingle was like the insect crawl of The Scout's feet. I looked back towards the door of the shelter where Minnie was sleeping but I didn't see anything.

The wet, yellow tape around the top of the Banks crackled and the voices I had heard in the Plant came back to me. I had heard the voices and listened but when I turned around Sharon had been standing in the cubicle with her hands over her ears and after that she was frightened. The voices faded down the corridor and I made her get through the window. As soon as we had climbed over the green railings she ran away. I didn't follow her.

I finished the cigarette. By that time the rain and sleet were coming down so hard you could barely see the Harbour. In other towns and cities it would be snowing. Close to the sea you only dreamed of snow, drifting into secret places.

I remembered the open bedroom window and the nightgown lifted over her private warmth. I started walking.

When I got to Mill Street I crossed the bridge and stopped at the chip van. I was the only one there. Empty chip bags blew about my feet as I waited. It was warm under the canopy and I listened to the radio.

But when I left the canopy the rain soaked the chips and the brown paper bag fell apart in my hands so I threw it in the gutter. I was passing the place where the bus depot used to be before a carbomb was put beside it. The bomb had sent corrugated iron from the roof flying over the town like fat, tin birds. The sound of tyres and paint cans exploding had lasted all night. Now the depot was just a compound with sodium lights, guard dogs and a high wire fence, but there was a wet, burnt smell that never left the place.

It hadn't been the only bomb in the town. Six months before that there had been a bomb at the telephone exchange and the explosion made every phone in the town ring madly at three in the morning like a pond full of black frogs.

But there hadn't been any bombs for a long time. The only things left were empty spaces and those cold ovens inside the gray landrovers. I put my head down and pulled my collar tighter around my neck with the sleet going past my skin, the touch of cold and tactile angels, winged bodies with women's legs, the feathered dexterous touch you imagine.

The car came towards me without dipping its headlights and I looked at the pavement because the light was burning my eyes. The car went past and I looked up again. Then I heard the wet slither of tyres as it did a tight, fast turn in the road behind. I started to run but it mounted the pavement just in front of me so that I ran into it and fell across the bonnet. My knees were numb from the impact against the front wing of the car and I felt sick. I heard a hubcap fall off

41

one of the wheels after it struck the kerb. The hubcap rolled across the road. It seemed to take a long time. From where I was lying across the bonnet I could see the headlights pointing against the wall of a shop beside the bus depot. There was only about a foot between the lights and the wall so that you could see every detail in the texture of the plasterwork, puckers and stretches like marks on skin, crossed by white flecks of rain and sleet. I could feel the heat of the engine through the bonnet. It made me feel sleepy.

They were in no hurry but when I heard the doors of the car open I knew I had to move. I slid off the bonnet. My legs took the weight and I put my back against the metal grille which covered the windows of the shop. They came in fast with the light behind them. The first kick missed my balls, sliding up into my stomach. The second one must have gone along my ribs.

They got in close and the fists started coming. I slipped down the grille and put my chin into my collar, making them strike from above, but that didn't last long. They lifted me and threw me face down across the bonnet. I felt kicks on my legs and punches on my kidneys.

One of them pulled me off the bonnet onto the ground.

"Keep your hands off her, Taig bastard", an unfamiliar voice said.

"Fenian get," another one said, and then there was one last kick in the ribs which made a noise like gristle when you cut it with a knife so that I felt my mouth open and a sound come out of it as if it was coming out of someone else's mouth.

The doors slammed and the car reversed away from me into the road, bumping and swaying as it left the pavement. The gears raked before the driver found first and drove away.

I lay in the street for a while with the side of my face pressed against the wet pavement. I could see where the sleet melted when it hit the pavement and I could feel water flowing through my fingers and around my cheek. The water felt warm, like bathwater.

TEN

There was no light in Sharon's bedroom but there was a car with one hubcap missing parked at her front door. I stood across the street in the doorway of a garage and waited. The wind made the plastic door behind me move with a booming noise and tore at my cigarette until the tip was a hot cone an inch long. From the house beside the garage I could hear the noise of a television. You couldn't make out the words, just distant noises like you hear through the walls of a strange room when you lie awake at night. Sounds like feet on a landing or a voice calling down the stairs or the slam of a door.

My face felt as if plaster had been moulded to it and then allowed to harden. Their fists had done that and the cold hadn't helped. On the way up the Avenue I had stopped to piss and the pain in my kidneys made me feel as if every drop was blood.

I watched the Venetian blinds at the front of Sharon's house. There was a light behind them but they didn't move. I stood there for over an hour but nothing moved except for papers filled with the wind and a piece of wire hanging loosely from a telegraph pole, tapping against a metal stanchion in a way that made you think of some kind of signal like morse in the wind that was so cold it seemed to blow between the inside of your ribs and your lungs.

When the front door of the house opened I had to use my sleeve to get rid of the tears the wind had pushed from my eyes.

Sharon's father stood in the doorway for a moment then he stepped aside to allow somebody out of the hall. Her father was younger than I expected, with the kind of moustache you see on policemen. He was in shirtsleeves and he kept his hands in his pockets, kicking his feet softly the way you do when you're talking to somebody at the door on a cold night.

43

I wasn't surprised to see Glennon there but I didn't expect his father. I recognised the black hair and the small eyes that you couldn't see for shadow. He got into the drivers seat of the car and started it. Sharon's father waved to him as he drove off.

Glennon must have said something funny because Sharon's father laughed and punched his shoulder gently. He shut the door and Glennon crossed the street, passing me with his face set against the wind and his breath streaming out behind him while I pressed back into the doorway as far as I could, trying to pull the shadow around me.

Later that night I found myself back at the Banks. I was walking along the path where you leaned sideways into the wind coming in from the sea until it dropped suddenly leaving you without gravity on the brink, weighted the wrong way and knowing how the stones and rubble on the beach below would hurt your bones like the cold getting through the enamel to the nerve in your teeth.

I looked over the cliff. All you could see was black water with white foam on it. The salt spray coming over the Harbour wall made my hair stick up in drenched nubs.

I was hoping for a fire at the shelter but it had gone out, although it was warm to put your hands on the stones around it. I squatted there and heard a throat being cleared followed by the sound of a spit.

I was in no hurry to go near Minnie, and the spit sounded like something pulled up from watery, dead lungs but I went to the other side of the shelter anyway and looked in through the small window there. There was no glass in the window so I pulled myself up to the level of the sill and looked in. At first I couldn't see or hear anything but then there was the sound that a bottle will make when it touches the ground. I wanted a drink so I went round to the doorway. When I was inside I struck a match.

Outside it was noisy but inside it was quiet except for the flush of water from the broken urinal and the ropes of spray that had started coming over the Banks to land on the roof. Minnie was sitting on the floor. I brought the match close to her face. She had her gut in her hand like some kind of famine victim and she was twitching and mumbling through her dentures.

44

I reached for the bottle that was sitting on the floor in front of her. The sweetness of VP sherry gluts your throat and stomach but it's not enough to warm you. She had seen the bottle disappear and she snatched it back.

"Would you jump into my grave as quick," she said. She belched and said pardon before she went on.

"Silk stockings would become your smooth calves," she said softly, "still and all I suppose there was no harm in him, not like some others I could name."

"Who?"

She tapped her stomach with a fingernail and gave me a sly look.

"Never you mind," she said.

I couldn't make head nor tail of it. She got up and went outside the way she did all the time. I lifted the bottle and took another drink. She stood in the doorway when she came back, looking up and down, then she came back and sat down heavily beside me. Suddenly she took my hand and stuck it under her coat. I could feel the pulled greasy wool of her cardigan under my fingers and beneath that her belly, hard as a nut, with ridges in it like iron. Her nails dug into me. She had a smell like old rinds.

"The man who done that to me," she said and I felt her hand chasing mine under the cardigan until she found it and pushed it against her stomach so hard the knuckles cracked.

I couldn't move. I felt as if she was going to burst me open against whatever secret she kept in that solid flesh.

"God child," she said then, "you're foundered with the cold." She tightened her grip until I was pressed against her old woman's boulder stomach and scraggy tits. I remembered a night during the Summer. I was standing in the carpark outside Cupids. There were other people in the carpark. It was a warm night. You could have heard someone laughing from a long way.

In one corner of the carpark there was a couple standing against the fence. He had his back to me and her face was almost invisible in the shadow. She was wearing a blouse with a loose neck which was pulled down at the side so that one breast was exposed.

I could see the long white gland clearly, as if it was floating on the air in front of my eyes, and as I looked I heard her laugh with a sound that filled my ears as if stars of ash were colliding a long way into space.

"Whisht," Minnie said, "Whisht now." Her grip relaxed so that she was holding me the way you would hold a child. I pushed her off me. She coughed and held her stomach. Outside the wind was loud and the sea slapped like wet leather against the stones on the beach and the concrete of the pier wall.

ELEVEN

That week it seemed as if there was nobody in the town any more. The wind carried slates from the warehouse into the river and made noise in the aerials on the coastguard station. In the morning there were always bottles and wet solids of puke in the gutters but you never saw who left them there. Up in the Desmesne there were parties at night. You heard the noise but you never saw anyone coming or going.

Deeds said it was like a town that was expecting an invasion. Saigon, Managua, one of those names you hear on television. Anyone with anything to lose has already left quietly at night. You didn't want to be among the ones that were left behind but you were.

I said that every time I walked through the town I got the kind of feeling you have when you wake up at night suddenly and you don't know where you are so that everything is strange and Deeds said that was right too.

The day after I got the hiding I was walking down Mill Street when I saw Deeds and Jammy on top of the loft. There was a strong east wind and you saw all sorts of things flying through the air. I saw a cloud of litter being blown towards me and in the middle of it was a woman's blouse, sleeves puffed with invisible flesh. I saw a plastic bin tumble all the way from the bridge to Cupids. All sorts of things. When I looked up and saw Deeds and Jammy up there I almost expected to see them take off from the roof, arms spread.

I climbed the ladder and found them putting a rope over the top of the loft to hold it down. I didn't ask them where they got the rope. Maybe it came there on the wind.

"Stop the lights," Jammy said when he saw my face.

"What happened to you?" Deeds asked.

"I was talking when I should have been listening," I said.

"Last night?" Deeds asked. I told them what had happened.

"Should have listened to your uncle Deeds," Deeds said.

"No flies on our Deeds," Jammy said.

Later Deeds asked me if I was seeing her again and I said that I didn't know. But later that evening I waited at the top of the Harbour road. When her shift ended I saw the white uniforms coming up the road in the fading light. She wasn't there.

Deeds and Jammy spent the next few days at the loft and at night Deeds brought Anne-Marie to the Avenue or up to the loft.

In the middle of the week I was standing on the corner of Mill Street and the Harbour road. I was in a shop front, out of the rain. A drainpipe emptied off the roof onto the pavement beside me making a noise like bare feet on wet tiles.

I must have been standing there for a long time with those feet running through my head. I didn't see the car until it had stopped at the kerb in front of me. The driver was invisible, but the passenger window was open and I saw Glennon staring at me, his big pale lips and small eyes, the skin around his eyes the same colour as his lips. He smiled at me. The top lip didn't move at one side when he smiled because there was still some swelling on it from Deeds fist. I backed into the doorway and waited for them to come at me, but Glennon just leaned his elbow on the car window and smiled.

"Now you know what happens to Taigs who go out with our girls," he said, "this is our town kid, and she belongs to us. If anybody's going to throw a shot into her I will."

I watched the car pull away from the kerb. When I took my hands out of my pockets they were scored red where the edge of the pocket had cut into my fist.

I crossed the street to the newsagents. The man in the shop had a bottom lip which stuck out. The lip was wet and there were shreds of tobacco on it. I bought cigarettes and he counted the change onto the counter. You could see the way the bones in his hand moved to make pockets of skin. There were yellow stains on his finger and thumb. When I reached for the change he gripped my arm.

"You see days like these," he said, "they could be the best days of our lives." Outside I looked up towards the loft and saw Sharon climbing the ladder towards it.

There was no sign of her on the roof. I went into the loft.

She didn't look around when I came in. There were pigeons all around her but she wasn't looking at them either. It was the pictures that interested her. Deeds had cut them from porn mags and stuck them to the wall of the loft. In the darkness the coloured squares of paper looked like rows of windows in which women were undressing.

"My da keeps a stack of them books in the garage," she said. She had her hands in the front pockets of her leather jacket so that the bones of her shoulders showed through the stretched leather. Her hair was greasy and flattened on one side as if she had slept on it.

"What are you doing here?" I asked. She shrugged and turned to face me putting her hands behind her back, palms pressed against the wall and her buttocks resting on her hands. Her eyes were black and her head was tilted so that you could see the blue shadows on her throat. When I touched her she was cold under her jacket and on her mouth.

She pushed me away and asked for a cigarette. I gave it to her and lit it, watching the way her eyelids fell as she bent forward, taking the light from my cupped hands with sipping breaths. The light from the match must have shone upwards into my face because her expression changed when she looked at me. She touched my cheek.

"Bastards," she said, "they had to tell me what they done to you. I near tore my da's eyes out and they wouldn't let me out of the house after that. I locked myself in the bathroom tonight and done a runner out the window."

She hesitated, dragging on the cigarette.

"I can't go back," she said, "I need someplace to go."

I thought about it. She went outside and walked to the edge of the roof. It was getting dark. You could see lighted windows in the Desmesne and streetlights going down towards the Harbour.

"You can see for miles," she said. She held her cigarette between finger and thumb as if she was sighting on a distant landmark, then she flicked it and watched it fall into the river below.

She couldn't stay at the loft but there was an old net store down at the Harbour. We climbed back down the side of the warehouse. I wondered how she had avoided Deeds traps. Later on I found out that you only fell into Deeds traps if you

49

wanted to.

I bought food on the way. She had a plastic bag with clothes in it. When we got to the Harbour we went around the inner basin, past the winches they used to unload the Polish boats. After that the tarmac road ran out and you were on dirt and stones. We reached the old boatbuilder's yard. Wooden buildings with tarred roofs. It was like walking through an ancient village. You expected old women in doorways, looking up at you when you passed, opening broken mouths wordlessly.

The net store was built on wooden piles over the water. Inside there were two skylights in the roof and torn nets on the rafters. There were holes in the plank floor and through the holes you could see the water beneath the building, black and glistening from diesel spillage.

Sharon took the food out of the plastic bag and set it out on the floor. For a while all you could hear was the sound of eating.

"I was starving," she said.

"What's the plan now," I said, "you can't stay here for long."

"Don't know."

"The roof is alright though," I said, "and you can sleep on the nets. Make them up into a bed."

"We could go away," she said.

I pulled some nets out of the rafters and piled them in the corner nearest the door. I stretched out on them. The place smelt of tar, wood and fish, and the water smelt of oil. She was watching me. The store was dark except for the Harbour lights which came through the skylights, so that if you stared at her it seemed as if the skin was sinking between the bones on her face.

She came over and sat down beside me, then she lifted her hand and touched my face again. Perhaps she had seen the same thing there. I brought her face closer to mine. She sucked my lip into her mouth. When she put her weight on top of me I could feel debris in the net pressed into my back. Shells, sea-urchins and starfish.

I stayed all night. You could stay there for ever, listening to the soft snaps and pulls of her breath, with the voices of the tide coming in underneath you, covering the mud and settling around the piles.

TWELVE

You imagine the feeling people must have had when they looked up and saw an airship for the first time. That anything so big could be light enough to float, all those silent miles of air, cable, canvas and rope.

It was the same when we woke up that morning and saw a big, Polish boat coming into the Harbour. I looked through a chink in the wall and all that was visible in either direction was the side of the ship. Green plates of steel and rivet heads brown with rust. You could barely tell that it was moving. There was just the sound of the engines and minute ripples at the waterline as if some small animal was digging itself into the Harbour bottom.

I went outside. The boat was taller than the Plant. They were using winches to bring it alongside the dock. As the stern swung round I could see to the other side of the inner basin. Deeds and Jammy were there. Even at that distance I knew what they were doing. They were waiting at the edge of the dock until a seagull flew past in the Harbour below them. Then they would try to bring it down with pieces of broken pallet or fishbox. They were easy to bring down. All you had to do was touch them.

I shouted across the inner basin. They waved to me and began to walk around the basin. I told Sharon that I wouldn't be long. I went as far as the Plant and waited for them beside the skips of fish guts that were left at the front of the Plant at the weekend. When the weather was hot the skips made a boiling sound and you could smell them all over the town.

But I heard a different kind of sound when I was standing there. I went to the back of the skips and I saw the Scout using his good hand to fork handfuls of the guts into a plastic bag.

"Puts lead in your pencil," he said, "and you'd need that in this town so you would if you seen the things I seen."

51

"What did you see?" Deeds asked as he walked up.

"Up in them new houses I seen things," the Scout said, "up in the Desmesne, nudie women running around all week."

"Don't talk shit," Deeds said.

"I seen it. Men with no faces."

"You're having us on," Deeds said.

"I've seen it," the Scout said, "they put sheets across the middle of the room with holes in them and the men put their dicks through the holes and the women pick and choose, squealing like pigs at the market. Men with no faces."

It wasn't the kind of market I imagined. I could see women moving among the secret stalls, handling the merchandise, blind roots, tubers of bliss.

Jammy giggled and the Scout put his head back and laughed so hard that you could see the back of his throat. His sick laugh. I could see the way he was holding the plastic bag, twisting it, his good hand working at the neck in a way that made me uneasy and the others must have noticed it as well because Jammy stopped giggling and Deeds eyes narrowed.

"We're no angels, are we boys?" The Scout's voice was like a hand on your throat and Deeds stepped forward with his fists clenched.

"Hard men," The Scout said, "hard as whores handbags."

Deeds looked at me. Nobody was laughing. The Scout held up the dripping plastic bag.

"None of youse joining me for a wee bite of dinner?"

He was gone then. You never knew how he could move so quickly.

"He's not the full shilling, yon boy," Jammy said.

We started to walk back towards the head of the inner basin where the river emptied into the Harbour. The tide was out and Jammy lobbed stones at bottles trapped in the black mud on the Harbour bottom. There was a smell like burnt rubber from the mud. Sometimes the stone would hit the iron pilings which supported the side of the dock, making a dull ring like a spoon on the side of a cup. Other times the stone would land in the mud, making a clean, triangular hole, darker than the surrounding mud.

When we reached the head of the basin we climbed down a concrete bank onto the riverbed. There was room to walk along the edge without stepping into the water until you reached the place where the concrete ended. Then there were two fields which were marked off for building land and you could walk through the fields until you reached the warehouses. There were trees overhanging the water with dried weed and plastic bags in their lower branches from floods. On the other side of the river you could see the backs of houses on the Harbour road. When the river flooded the water could rise to the level of the back windows and deposit parcels of mud and silt smelling of meat in ground floor rooms. But that hadn't happened for a long time.

Further up the river there was a place where the water had cut away a high bank, leaving a small cliff with a tree on top. One of the branches of the tree jutted out over the river and there was a rope attached to it.

I went up first. I took my jacket off and used it to lasso the rope. There was a knot at the end of the rope and I put one foot on the knot and pushed with the other so that I went spinning out over the river fifty feet below.

At the arc of the swing you could see all the way down the river to the Harbour. You could see all the roofs, gutters and gables of the town. You could see the silver roof of the Plant and you could see the new, gray roofs of the houses in the Desmesne. You could see towns without people, or with people so small they were only the size of a fingernail.

The rope rotated so that I could see down between the red brick houses on the Harbour road where the pavement wasn't wide enough to wheel a pram. The wind had subsided during the night and the air was still. There was smoke from chimneys hanging in the air between the houses. Some children were pulling a bogey made of an old fish box and bicycle wheels along the road. The fish box contained lemonade bottles half-filled with silt. The children found them in the river and brought them back to the shop for the deposit. Further on down the road the pavement was chalked off for hopscotch and some girls were bouncing a tennis ball off a gable and singing.

I could make out The Submarine as well. Ann-Marie was outside washing the windows. She had a plastic bucket and a cloth. When she lifted her arm out of the bucket it was red and steaming because of the cold air. When she reached towards the glass it was as if I could see along the white underside of her arm to the wet curled darkness of her armpit. Every time her arm passed over the glass I could feel the soft grunt she made in the back of her throat.

I was getting tired. If you didn't keep enough momentum going on the swing it slowed down until eventually you couldn't step back onto the top of the cliff. If that happened the only thing you could do was to hold on until you couldn't hold on any longer and then just drop off into the river below where the water was shallow.

I got off onto the bank and Deeds got on. Deeds could swing higher than any of us. He stayed up there for a long time, jack-knifing on the rope, the rope coughing against the branch, his body making the sound of wings as it went through the air, swinging higher than the rest of us until he could see onto the roof of the warehouse where the door of the loft was unlocked when it shouldn't be and was swinging backwards and forwards in a breeze which you couldn't feel at ground level, opening and closing on a doorway as dark as the Scout's throat.

The rope twitched as Deeds checked it at the high point of the swing, destroying the momentum so that he had to dive for the bank on the back swing, losing his footing then picking himself up and running for the river.

We followed him, running upstream through the water, our feet slipping on the greasy rocks, the ladder on the side of the warehouse swaying under our weight, the tiles on the roof slithering.

You've seen footage of great disasters on television with the victims laid out on the floor of an aircraft hangar or school gym, covered in blankets. It was like that. The pigeons were lined up in neat rows, each one with its neck broken and a tiny bubble of dried blood on its beak. Jammy stood there with a red face and his hands in his pockets looking down at the birds as if it was a trick where you lifted the right bird and you found a coin or a tiny, beating heart underneath.

Deeds didn't seem to look at the birds. He had the same expression on his face as he did the time he fought Glennon.

After a long time he began to lift the birds and carry them to the edge of the roof, one by one. He didn't say a word. Jammy stood at the door of the loft, watching him, then he

54

went to the edge of the roof and looked over. He walked back to the loft, put his head against the door and started to cry.

Deeds carried all the birds to the edge. It was very quiet. All you could hear was the voices of girls playing hopscotch on the Harbour road below. And when Deeds dropped the birds off the edge of the roof their ounces of flesh and hollow bone made no noise as they fell.

THIRTEEN

Deeds arranged to meet Haresy and JB in the Harbour cafe at four o'clock. We met them on the way there and went into the pool room. JB put money in the pool table and poured the pool balls, jolting, into the wooden triangle.

"So Glennon's for it," he said. Deeds screwed the blue chalk onto the tip of his cue and rolled the white ball onto the edge of the ruined, felt crescent.

"The heavy dint," Haresy said. Anne-Marie came in and began to wipe tables. Deeds placed the sucked welt of his cigarette carefully on the rim of the table without looking at her. Outside the sky was blue, darkening as the sun went down. Frost had begun to show white on the black tarred roof of the loft by the time we came down to the ground, leaving Jammy there.

"You should have fucking done him the first time," Haresy said, "them birds were worth a fortune."

"They hang around the top of the Avenue after Cupids," JB said, "there's only a couple of them usually. We could do it then."

"His own ma won't know him," Haresy said.

"Alright," Deeds said, "tonight."

"Is he in on it," Haresy said, jerking his head at me.

"Why wouldn't he?" Deeds said. Haresy didn't look in my direction.

"Things get around," he said, "he goes out with that wee Prod from the Desmesne, and her da hangs out with Glennon."

"There's no law against a Prod going out with a Taig," Deeds said.

"I seen the two of them up at the loft last night," Haresy said.

"Wise up," Deeds said so softly you could barely hear him.

"I hear tell them Prods ride like rabbits," Haresy said. He

56

laughed and walked quickly and noiselessly around the table until he was standing behind Deeds. He put his hands on Deeds back and castored on his hips, thrusting his crotch into Deeds buttocks.

"Black hole," he said, "nothing like it." Deeds pounded the butt of the cue into his stomach and turned, holding the cue by its tip. His face was white. Haresy fell back against the wall.

"I was only messing," he said.

"We'll meet at the Banks, eleven tonight," Deeds said.

Deeds went back to the loft where Jammy was still sitting where we had left him. Wide-awake and listening to the eggs whispering to each other in their cold nests.

I thought about what Haresy had said on my way back to the net store. I thought about Glennon wetting his lips. I thought about those gray landrovers, Sharon spilling her brief language onto the metal floor.

The big Polish boat filled the Harbour with lights. There was a smell of coffee. Men were moving about on the upper decks and there was music coming from somewhere.

She looked frightened when I pushed open the door of the net store. She was sitting at the far end of the building on the edge of one of those big holes in the floor. When she saw it was me she looked back down at the water. I sat down beside her.

"I was just thinking," she said, "you know the way you look at the water and it's the same water everywhere. Like if you went to the other side of the sea it would still be the same water."

I knew what she meant. The same black water burning against chunks of floating ice and against coral and sandy beaches in the night.

"Like when you look at the sky," she said, "it's the same so it is, doesn't matter where you are in the world."

She sounded like Binty. I told her what had happened to the pigeons.

She was sitting with her hands between her thighs and her eyes reflecting the colour of the water, returning its blackness through a hole in the world.

"Did you hear the music," she said.

"What?"

"The music. I listened to it all night waiting for you to come back. I thought something had happened."

"Why didn't you tell me that you knew what Glennon had done to Binty? You knew that he didn't fall over the Banks. You knew that Glennon did it and his da covered up.

"Take me away from here," she said quietly, "I'm going to die here."

"Tell me why?"

"You know nothing," she shouted, "please can we go, please?"

Every so often a car goes over the edge of the dock and into the Harbour. The last time it happened you could see the skid marks leading up to the dock and the car headlights under the water. That happens sometimes. The headlights stay on until water gets into the electrics.

I was there when they lifted the car out using a crane. There was a frogman in the water. When the car cleared the surface a lot of water ran out of it at first but by the time it got to the level of the dock there was very little.

I saw a young couple sitting upright in the front seat. The car was swinging and tilting slowly on the chains and you could hear the noise that the generator and the crane made, but everybody on the dock was very quiet as if they could hear the silence in the car as it sat on the Harbour bottom, two pairs of eyes staring through the windscreen to where the headlights opened the darkness like a door opened onto an empty room.

We stared at the water in silence for a long time. When I got up to go I felt her touch my arm.

"I swear I never," she said, "I swear."

But she didn't go on. Outside I zipped up my jacket. I had forgotten how cold it was.

FOURTEEN

I recognised the car that was parked in the Esplanade car park. My knees had left shallow dents in the front wing. I put my hand on the bonnet where the lacquer was warm and smooth.

I recognised the voice that had spoken in the Plant that night. Albert Glennon was on his hunkers in front of Minnie. From the doorway of the shelter I saw his hair oiled back over the skull and the scalp showing white between the black strands like dead skin, the nose and the thin lips. His eyes were sunk into shadow, or pulled into shadow like a glove pulled inside out.

"I seen him do it," Minnie said, "I knew him for a son of yours. He's the spit of you by the face."

"You've a hard heart," he said.

"Hard heart my arse and me never saying a word this twenty-five year about the way you left me and never seen hide nor hair of you since. Mind you I'd rather not have the child if it ended up like thon skitter, or like you. You never gave me a red cent for ripping out my insides for you."

"Are you sure you saw him Minnie?"

"I saw your son kicking Binty."

"I'll say he was up at the house that night. Your word against mine Minnie. The man's voice was soft like bad meat."

"Aye, your word and mine. Never fear I'll go to no police barracks telling tales about your son. Sure who would credit me anyway. You have the law in your pocket."

"I knew you'd see sense Minnie. You're a sensible girl."

I saw him change position. One of his hands held her wrist and the other hand rose to her face. I watched it fan there like breath. It stayed for a moment then it dropped to her neck.

"You're a sensible girl Minnie," he said again. His voice was cold and hollow. I could see the broad, flat tips of his fingers and the nails coloured by the freezing, watery light in the shelter, the rubbery wattles of her neck rubbed smooth under the fingers so that you could almost hear the rustle of blood and breath in the skin. I wanted to shout out to her but I couldn't.

"Just a wee touch Minnie," he said, "you're a sensible girl."

One hand went from her neck to the opening of her cardigan. It entered quickly, disappearing into the wool. His other hand was working at his crotch. The zip slid down. It was the sound of a thousand, small mouths chewing, oozing silk.

I left the shelter and didn't go back, even when Albert Glennon left, walking on to the Esplanade without looking right or left, starting his car and driving off. But once you hear the kind of noises two people make together you never forget them.

Deeds arrived alone. I started to tell him everything but I kept quiet when I realised that he wasn't listening. When I stopped talking he looked at me.

"You look like you've seen a ghost," he said. It made me feel uneasy. He handed me a bottle of vodka and I took a long drink.

Haresy and JB arrived about five minutes later. I handed the bottle to JB. While he was drinking Haresy took a Stanley knife out of his pocket and swung it at stomach level.

"Gut the bastard," he said, smiling with his broken mouth. He put the knife back into his pocket. JB handed him the bottle. When he drank the liquid ran out of the corners of his mouth. Deeds looked over at me. His smile came and went like smoke.

"Come on and get it over with," he said.

"Where's Jammy?" JB asked.

"I couldn't find him," Deeds said.

"Who needs him," Haresy said, touching his pocket.

It was cold. We crossed the Esplanade. You could see the lights of Mill Street up ahead.

"Looks like a border," Deeds said, pointing at the double row of streetlights. He was thinking that we were walking towards a border without passports, wondering if you could break out, climb the barbed wire, cross the brightly lit strip without stepping on the freshly dug patches that would conceal mines. Hoping that the guards were asleep in their watchtowers, or sitting in warm guardrooms passing around snapshots of their wives, children, sweethearts.

Our feet made a snapping noise on the pavement. Behind me I could hear Haresy chapping his hands against the cold.

We turned the corner onto Mill Street. When it is cold like that everything else is suppressed so that you can hear the silence of lifeless things in your head and see ghost shapes of cars, lamp posts and people caught in frost.

We stood behind the wall at the top of the Avenue and waited for Cupids to end. We waited for a long time. There were no couples walking up the Avenue from Cupids but when you had waited that long you started to imagine silent couples pinned to each tree with frost, clothes and skin stiff with it.

We heard the noises that meant Cupids was over. Someone whispering, someone crying, a shadow of vomit on the ground.

The noises stopped. There was no sign of Glennon. Ice cracked in the branches of the trees behind us. The noise of a bird's small heart frozen in flight.

In the end Deeds straightened his legs and stood up.

"He's not coming," he said. He lit a cigarette and shivered. Haresy and JB stood up as well. Haresy said something under his breath. JB said something back. I didn't look round. Then Haresy was in front of me, pointing his finger in my face. I had been waiting for this.

"Glennon knew about this from the start so he did," he said, "you fucking told him. You're hand in glove with that lot, you and your black cunt, even showed her the way to the loft."

Haresy turned to Deeds who hadn't moved.

"He's a squealer so he is," he said. Deeds shook his head slowly and dragged on his cigarette. JB didn't move. Haresy looked back at me. He had his hand in his pocket. I backed out of the Avenue gates slowly and Haresy followed. The Stanley knife came out of his pocket.

"That black bitch," he said, "you'd eat a mile of her shite to get up her hole."

As he came towards me I remembered the way Sharon had come to the shelter on the night Binty had been killed and how she had wanted to take me away because she must have known that Glennon was looking for one of us. She couldn't warn me. You get a habit of silence in this town.

Haresy brought the knife up from the level of his waist. I could see rust on the blade. I caught his wrist and used his own momentum to spin him around. I pushed him across the pavement in front of me with his arm forced up his back until he collided with a parked car. A wing mirror broke off its stem with a chipped sound, leaving just the chrome stem pointing upwards like a long fingernail, the cuticles stripped.

We just stood like that for a minute. Haresy was drawing long bubbling breaths through his split mouth. All I wanted to do was to get to the net store.

Haresy twisted out of my hands. I reached for him again. He jumped and landed on the bonnet of the car. I stopped moving and watched the way his feet started to slip on the bonnet which was white with frost. Through the windscreen I saw someone in the passenger seat light a cigarette. The match flared and the shadow fell between the lips and the eyes. Haresy's feet went out from under him. You could see which way he was going to fall, but it took a long time before his face dipped towards the stem of the wing mirror, his head bowed as if he was drinking. There was no sound. The bone socket of his eye fitted the metal and then there was just the chrome again, dark this time.

The next thing I remember is Deeds pulling me to my feet and forcing me to run through the gate of the Avenue. JB just looked after us and smiled. We turned off the Avenue and into the trees. Behind us I could hear Haresy shouting.

"I'm blinded, I'm fucking blinded." We slid into the bottom of a ditch. Old bottles and plastic bags caught in frozen water crunched like birds skulls under our feet. We climbed onto a wall and jumped down onto the other side.

It was a moment before I realised that we were in McConville's yard. There were steel pens in front of us and a long low shed beyond that. There was a single bulb on the outside of the shed and you could see where the yard sloped to a drain with an iron cover.

We walked into the middle of the yard. It was slippery where it had been washed and the water had turned to ice. The light from the bulb was brittle. We couldn't hear Haresy any more. Our breath spilled out like soft voices into the empty pens and the shed.

Deeds went towards the shed. I saw him disappear inside the open doors. He called to me.

Inside the shed it was bright. There were only a few lights but the walls were painted white. On each side of the building there was a metal rail with meathooks every few feet. The rails went all the way to the back of the building. Under the rails there were channels cut in the concrete floor. The floor was dark and wet and the hooks were bare.

Deeds leaned forward to touch a chain which was attached to one of the hooks. The rail shook and all the hooks moved at once, heavily as if they were hung with invisible carcasses, jostling each other and dripping into the gutters.

Deeds touched the chain again and all the hooks shook their whitened tips and the shed filled with noise.

FIFTEEN

By the time I got to the net store that night I knew that it was too late. The small door at the side was open. You expect to see signs of a struggle. A door swinging on broken hinges, tables and chairs overturned, blood perhaps. But an unwashed cup or food wrappers lying on the table or clothes tangled in the pile of nets is violence enough to convince you.

I walked across to the nets. There was a black room between the floorboards and the water beneath. My feet echoed in it. I picked up a teeshirt from the pile of clothes. It smelt of nets. I found a pair of jeans with panties balled in the crotch. The panties had a comb of lace on the front and around the legs like the lips of an anemone. They were cold and stiff.

"You'll not find her in there at any rate," the Scout said. His uneven footsteps followed me across the floor.

"She's long gone, back to daddy, I'd say." I thought about the last time I'd seen her, hunched and frozen.

"She's warm enough," he said. Then I imagined one of those landrovers drawn up outside the net store. Sharon climbing into the back, the noise the doors made as they closed and the small square of greenish bulletproof glass that you couldn't see through from the outside.

"Nobody took her," the Scout said, "left of her own free will so she did." I turned to look at him and I saw what had happened. Glennon standing in the doorway of the net store. Sharon watching him in the darkness. Her feet inaudible on the floor when she joined him. She didn't look once at the Polish boat as they walked around the inner basin.

"Now there's a thing for you," the Scout said, "I wouldn't have believed it if I hadn't seen it with my own two eyes."

I still had the jeans in my hand. I threw them away so that they slipped through one of the holes in the floor and fell through without noise as if they hadn't touched water but had kept on falling. When I turned the Scout had gone.

SIXTEEN

Deeds used to say that words leave shadows in your mind and Binty used to talk about the city where they dropped the first bomb. How people were sitting on doorsteps and walking on the pavements. The sun must have been shining. They heard planes but they didn't look up because they heard planes every day. Sparrows sat on telegraph poles and pigeons flew along the rivers, staying close to the walls on either side. The pavements were dusty, dreaming of rain. And then the stars collapsed and turned to ash. The hot wind collected the ash and took it away and there were shadows of people sitting on doorsteps, walking on the pavement. Their shadows were printed on the ground and the ashes rustled in the wind and were gone.

Jammy wasn't missed until the next day and it was Deeds who found him, floating face-up in the river downstream from the warehouses.

Everyone assumed that he had stumbled into one of Deeds traps and the police had put incident tape across the river. I found Deeds down at the Banks.

He told me how he'd found Jammy wedged between rocks with his head pointing downstream, the current rolling it from side to side as if he was being interrogated by an invisible hand. The blood had drained from his face so that his complexion was clear and his hair streamed out behind him. Deeds swore he looked beautiful. Then he told me that Jammy hadn't slipped. The other thing had never occurred to me.

Words leave shadows in your mind. Deeds talked so that his voice was soft like wings alighting on the tin roofs and slates and gutters and telegraph wires of the town. He told me about the first night he had brought Anne-Marie to the loft and how he had stayed on her until the whole loft shook and the pigeons were dislodged from their perches like big fruit, soft in their panic with their wings thudding against the wooden walls. They lay awake in the silence afterwards, her eyes open in the dark, a packet of Frenchies scattered on the floor glowing like silkworms and Deeds smoking with the cigarette cupped in his hand and butts stubbed out in the lid of a paint can on the floor.

Other nights Deeds would sit on his own at the edge of the roof. Sometimes, he said, the town would be noisy at night, sounds coming up from locked bedrooms as if you were on the other side of a thin wall in a strange room and heard a man's voice and then a woman's. On nights like that the lights in the Desmesne would seem to burn until morning. Sometimes it would be quiet and he would watch the town dwindle and empty.

On a quiet night he climbed the ladder and looked into the loft. Jammy was asleep on the floor with one hand on a wicker basket which had a pigeon's beak coming out of an airhole on the side.

Deeds walked back onto the roof and stood at the edge. He told me he felt as if he could have lifted the loft without waking Jammy, put it on the palm of his hand and blow lightly then watch it float over the edge, going downriver towards the sea and weaving when the wind brushed it.

I wanted to know what else he had seen from the loft. You could have seen anything from there. But when I turned he was gone and I remembered what he had said about being invisible.

SEVENTEEN

The rain began after dark. You stand at the edge of the Banks looking out at the sea and at the Harbour where the arc lights come on all at once and you wait as if you're waiting for a signal but it doesn't come, or at least not from the direction you expect.

When the rain began I turned and went back to the shelter. The rain was inside my collar and running down my back. When I got to the shelter I saw Sharon inside, hunched on one of the benches with her legs drawn up so that her heels touched the point of her buttocks and her chin rested on her knees.

It was almost as if I had suddenly seen Binty, his mouth reeling stories like silk through the dead emptiness. I stood there for a long time. She didn't look at me or say anything at first. I sat down beside her. I could feel the rain seeping through my jacket and I realised that she hadn't been there for long because her hair was wet and when she moved her arm I saw how the material of her blouse left a shadow of water on the wall so that she would be cold to touch.

"I'm afraid," she said.

"I know."

"You don't know," she said, "you weren't there when I came back last night."

The night that Binty was killed, she said, she was upstairs when she heard Glennon tell her father that he was going to the Banks to wait for Deeds or me. Glennon saw her and pushed her back against the wall digging his thumb into her eye and told her to keep her mouth shut and her father laughed.

Then I had left her alone in the net store. Glennon found her there. He had reached it just as we were leaving the Banks to wait for him outside Cupids.

Afterwards she lay on the nets for a long time. She could

see the two cups that we had used to drink from on the first night. The shape of mouths on the rim of each obliterated by arclights from the Harbour shining through the roof.

"He hurt me," she said. She unbuttoned her blouse. There were braided marks on her neck and ribs. Nailmarks on her breasts. Her nipples were hard and cold like small stones.

But then it wasn't the first time she had been hurt. Those magazines her father kept in the garage. The colour pages that were still sticky when you touched them. And then you see your father and the thing you remember is that there is hair growing in his nose and ears, not that his hands are rising like water around your calves, filling the space between heartbeats, rustling in the hollows at the back of your knees.

She put her arm around my waist and her head on my chest so that I could feel the small, wet hairs on her temple and when I pressed my chin down to hold her I could detect the light, mobile bone of her skull underneath her hair. Her mouth moved against my chest. She had allowed Glennon to kiss her so that when she suggested that they go to the Plant he had followed her without question.

She kissed me again. I opened my eyes when I felt her mouth against mine. In the darkness there was the round blue bulb that her eye made under the skin of the eyelid. I had one hand on her ribs feeling her heart's noise. Her tongue was in my mouth. Flat, strong muscle stroking the ridges of my palate, her heart's fat animal of chambers and valves moving faster. I took my mouth away from hers.

"Why did you go to the Plant?" She shrugged.

"I'll show you," she said.

When we came out from behind the coastguard station I could see the Polish boat forming a fence of lights across the Harbour. The tide was in and black water came through the narrow channel at the pier, filling the inner basin to the brim, pushing fish heads up the river, past the warehouses and the back walls of houses on the Harbour road and under the bridge. You imagined the Harbour filling until fish heads began to burst through floorboards in the town.

The rain came on the east wind across the Harbour wall to blow flat on the dock and the water. The bollards along the edge of the basin were dark and wet. There was a chip van on the edge of the dock. You could see the steam from it being blown down towards the concrete where it seemed to stop for a moment before the wind caught it again and made it disappear.

She slid down the slope behind the coastguard station, turning to urge me on when she got to the bottom, the wind making shapes in the wet material of her blouse.

I lost my footing on the slope and landed on an old fish box which cracked and splintered under my weight but I didn't lose sight of the white blouse, the tiny, perfect organs of her shoulderblades beating inside it as she walked away.

The Plant had been closed for the weekend. The compound was full of lorry trailers that would be taken away on Monday morning. You could feel the noise of their diesel cooling units in the ground under your feet.

Sharon climbed the fence. She pulled up her skirt to clear the spikes. There was rust and flakes of paint at the top of each spike. I saw one of them make a dent in the round flesh on the inside of her thigh. She stayed like that for a moment, with one leg on either side of the fence, looking down at me. A gust of wind made her hair cover her face. I could see the outline of each small tooth in her smiling mouth.

She could have been naked. She climbed down. When we reached the broken window she put her finger to her lips as if the need for silence had never been so strong. Standing under that window you couldn't have made a noise if you tried.

Inside you couldn't hear the noise of the diesel engines any more. There was just the water, the mirrors and the porcelain. She waited for me to climb through the window and then she took my hand.

"You have to shut your eyes," she said, as if it was going to be a surprise. I looked at her.

"Shut your eyes," she said, "shut them."

From the light that came through my eyelids I guessed that she was taking me along the corridor where the lamps were like moths. There was a smell of fish, organs, oil and scales. She was humming as she walked. The sound made me feel cold. She slowed down and the doors at the end of the corridor slapped open.

"Careful," she said, when the doorframe brushed my shoulder. Her hand held mine softly. The light was harsher

69

on the floor of the Plant. There was the smell of machinery and fish and another smell that you noticed on everyone in this town.

"You can open your eyes now," she said, but I didn't open them immediately. First of all I thought about Sharon when she was asleep on the pile of nets. The shape she made with one palm open by her face and her breathing like voices in an empty room.

I opened my eyes. I had never been so close to someone who was dead. You expect a corpse like that to look surprised, but Glennon didn't look surprised. You could tell that he had been dead for a while. Instead of the surface of his eye being glass-coloured it was crumpled like the wing of a fly.

The body was lying beneath the wooden slab where Sharon worked. There was a pool of yellowish urine between its legs. You lie awkwardly when you're dead.

Sharon was looking at it as if it was a crack that had opened in the floor but when her eyes reached the filleting knife in the ribs they started to open the way eyes, mouths, cunts open when they see something they recognise.

Glennon must have wondered why she brought him there. His look as she approached him, that walk, silently on the balls of her feet, crushed hair, eyelids, breasts moving, the moist press, the knife held in fingertips that were drops of milky water.

We could have stayed there for ever with the wind banging on the factory roof. Three mouths fixed on what it's like to die. No black car, windows opening with a soft whine, or a perfect hand laying flowers.

Glennon must have been very still when the knife entered. Suddenly attentive, all eyes and ears. You could see that when you looked at the body. No detail would have been to small. But I didn't feel that way. Everything was distant. Not that anything had changed but that I was standing a long way off, invisible, inaudible. But Sharon's mouth and eyes were open as if an invisible hand had gripped and twisted her skull, stretching the skin back from the eyes and forehead and forcing the jaw to open.

I hadn't heard the door open, but when I looked around I saw Albert Glennon standing between Sharon and me. His eyes were narrowed. His head swung to look at each of us, balanced on the point of each swing then dropped until he was looking at the body again. He stayed like that for a while, breathing heavily, a heartbeat in the jowl.

"What happened?" he asked. The voice was tiny in a pouch of fat that was pink and raw. No-one answered.

"I warned him," he said. He looked at Sharon for a long time then he turned to me, lifting an eyebrow. I went over to Sharon.

"I have to go now." She nodded. Her eyes were tired and black with the lethal cosmetics of the blood.

"One of ours," he said, still looking at the body. When I left they were still standing there, neither moving nor touching.

EIGHTEEN

There is a way of holding a petrol bomb when you throw it so that the petrol doesn't spill down your arm. You don't overfill it and you hold it the correct way.

Deeds taught me that. The time after they blew up the bus depot we spent an afternoon on the roof of the warehouse making petrol bombs. Deeds put sugar into the petrol so that it would stick like napalm, he said, and have the same sweet, oily smell. There was a warm breeze that day and you could almost smell the jungle's hot rain and insects.

He filled a whole crate with petrol bombs and hid them down at the Harbour. One of these days, he said, he was going to burn the whole town to the ground, walk along the street and destroy it the way he destroyed it in his mind every day with fountains of dust and fire following him, doorframes and plate glass bulging and splitting, loaves of bread, television sets, plastic bags and magazines spilling onto the street and people blown naked, tumbling limbs on the street, jackets blouses and skirts flapping in useless breezes above the town.

While we were in the Plant Deeds had gone to the Glennon house, following the tarmac drive as it made a crescent between two kerbs of granite whose grit of mica would soon be glittering in reflected light. He had gone to the front of the house. Maybe he walked on the lawn because the drive became gravel there and small stones might spatter to break the silence.

Maybe he stood there for a long time, suddenly attentive, rain on his glasses and the wire frames cold to touch. Somewhere else in the town curtains are drawn and screens begin to flicker behind them with a blue light. Or someone is taking the film from the back of an instamatic camera, waiting for the film to dry, gripping its sticky wetness between finger and thumb until it is dry as it will ever be and

72

she looks at you from the photograph and her eyes say yes before you have a chance to black out the face until it is beyond help.

There is a way of holding a petrol bomb when you throw it so that the petrol doesn't spill down your arm. Deeds stood outside the Glennon house striking matches in the rain until the wick of the petrol bomb caught properly.

Deeds went up in flames on the lawn of the Glennon house, the petrol igniting with a soft sound like the wind in silk, smooth as handled limbs, illuminating eyes hidden in haunted shadows, feathers on shoulderblades and bellies, the soft sounds they made to themselves.

When I came out of the Plant I saw the Scout sitting on the bonnet of Albert Glennon's car. The hand in the black, leather glove rattled against the car and made the noise of all his dark walks, the sound of small cries under the trees of the Avenue at night, men with hungry faces and stripping fingers, women with sad, voracious eyes hanging skindeep, white sheets.

We saw the flames in the town, orange in the rain and low cloud. We stood there watching them. The cables holding the Polish ship creaked, lifting sheets of water as they tightened in the swell. I remembered what Deeds had said about putting the loft to his lips and blowing it towards the sea. You imagined the Polish boat slipping its moorings, climbing with lights.

When I looked away from the boat I saw the Scout grinning and twisting one hand against the other as if he was wringing a neck and I understood what had happened to the pigeons.

NINETEEN

Every animal has a homing instinct, Deeds used to say.
Some bright magnet in the flesh. That must have been the
way I got from the Harbour to the path along the top of the
Banks. I heard two sirens from the direction of the town. As
soon as the sirens started there was movement and jolting
noises from the cars parked in the Esplanade car park. I
didn't realise what it was at first and I remembered how
Jammy wouldn't touch the coffins in the old graveyard
because he said that sometimes they dug up a coffin and
found long nailmarks on the inside of the lid. That meant
that whoever was in the coffin wasn't really dead when they
were buried. You woke up and it was completely dark and you
couldn't move. Binty said that your nails and hair kept on
growing after you were dead.

But when I heard the first engine start I knew what was
happening. The noise I had heard was people climbing out of
the back seats of the cars, zips being quickly fastened, skirts
smoothed, damp panties being stuffed into handbags beside
combs, lipstick, tissues and mirrors.

They would follow the ambulances as far as the Glennon
house and the Plant and wait for them to load the bodies, one
of which would be stiff and wettish and the other
incandescent.

You imagined what the Esplanade would be like after that.
Black with cars, their springs ticking.

"God child," Minnie said, when I looked into the toilets and
saw her on the floor, "you're soaked to the skin. I don't know
why in the name of god you go around in the rain like that.
You're not half-wise. Come in out of the rain like a good
child."

I sat down beside her and she handed me a bottle. I
shivered when the wine touched my throat.

"Take her easy," she said, pulling the bottle out of my

hand. "I'm starved for the bit of company these days with poor Binty gone. Not that he was the full shilling anyway. Then there was that poor friend of yours that fell off the roof. Break your heart so it would. If he was a child of your own you wouldn't feel any worse, not that I've any worry on that score and maybe I'm as well off."

Down at the Harbour the yellow lights burned as if there were acres of barbed wire underneath and a smell of burning. If you looked closely you could see the blue lights of an ambulance.

"You think I don't know the stories they tell about me in this town. Mind you I put lead in many a man's pencil but you wouldn't be up to the class of people you get in this town, the stories they come up with."

She took a long drink from the bottle and put her hands to her stomach.

"Albert frigging Glennon," she said slowly and I noticed for the first time that her voice was weak, "he said he'd pay me to get rid of the child and not a red cent did I ever see. But he's paid me now."

I realised that I hadn't seen her for days. I leaned forward and touched her. She was taut and her belly was as hard as a barrel of cement. She must have been sitting there since the day that Albert Glennon had come to her and started the memory of her baby ticking in her stomach like a fat clock. She started to groan as if she was going to spread her legs and have the ghost of a baby in front of my eyes.

TWENTY

The day before Deeds funeral I went down to the netstore. The door was open and it moved in the wind. Under the building the incoming tide was beginning to cover the mud, its small fingers and thumbs surrounding the wooden pilings as if they were about to prise them out of the Harbour bottom.

The place was empty. Her clothes had gone. Even the shape of her body in the nets had disappeared. I waited. You always wait for something. Like when you stand at the back of a funeral and wait for the sound of heels on the gravel behind you and the crowd between you and the grave opens with a moan. You don't look up but you know that the stranger's calves will whisper like silk as she walks and that she won't lift her veil and that her hands will be long and beautiful.

She had taken the debris out of the nets and left it on a shelf. I handled each piece. Starfish, sea-urchins, crab claws. I put them to my face and inhaled the way you do when you've spent the night with someone and next day you put the tips of your fingers to your nostrils.

When I had done that I walked over to the hole in the floor and sat down on the edge where I had seen her sit. The Polish freighter had left early the morning after we had been in the Plant and no-one had seen Sharon since so that I wondered if the black water underneath me was beneath her feet and I wondered if she had stood on the deck and looked back at the town.

Then I saw something light-coloured in the mud at the edge of the water. It was hard to make out. It was one of the cups which had been standing on the table in the net store. I remembered the shape of her lips on the rim. I wondered if the black water was rising over her, cupping the hollow of her jaw, obliterating the blue shadow and filling her mouth.

76

Later I walked up the river to the warehouse. The door of the loft was open as well. Inside the door the wall was dark with rain and Deeds magazine pictures tugged at the tacks which held them. You could see feathers trapped between the boards of the wall which moved in the draught. There were pigeon droppings on the floor.

I imagined the way it would have been on the night that the Scout killed the pigeons. The birds streaming in a circle around his head while he stroked them one by one from the air. Wingbeats getting fainter against the frayed, black cuffs of his jacket. Before he laid them out in rows he must have folded the broken wings like gloves to cover the breasts and pink feet.

I walked onto the roof and looked downriver towards the Harbour. Behind me the door of the loft opened and closed in the wind the way doors in deserted towns open and close to remember their population.

The day of the funeral was still and cold. I stood at the back of the crowd. There was gravel under my feet. I could hear ropes slapping against the wood of the coffin. I looked behind me and saw Anne-Marie standing between the headstones. She was wearing a black skirt and a white blouse under a black jacket. There was a veil pinned to her hair. All the women were wearing veils.

I stayed behind in the graveyard after the funeral. Two men strolled up with shovels, rolled up the artificial grass and started to fill in the grave. I heard earth strike the coffin and felt as if they were throwing everything in. Fish heads, old prams, grass clippings, builders rubble, old bottles. Anything to make him stay down there. I left them to it and began to walk back towards the town.

TWENTY ONE

The next time I saw Minnie she was lying on her back in a hospital bed with her eyes closed. Her mouth was open. Every time her chest rose and fell there were half-breaths and whistles. The gray cuffs of her hair lay on the white pillow like ash. Her head didn't dent the pillow as if she didn't weigh anything any more. The part of her eyelid that only shows when you are asleep was white and soft. Her belly supported the blankets and her knees were raised.

She was attached to a monitor by wires. Apart from her breathing the machine was the only other noise in the ward. I wondered what happened to the machine at night when there was no one else around. If it would sometimes show two heartbeats instead of one. The thick blue line I could see now and the bird's heartbeat of a child.

I stayed there for a long time but her eyes didn't open and the sound of her breathing didn't change. The light faded outside and no one came in to turn on the ward lights so that it was as if her face was being covered with water and you could no longer see the blackheads and broken veins. The way Jammy was beautiful for a moment and then invisible.

Outside it didn't seem as dark. I turned at the gates of the hospital and looked back. Minnie was in one of the prefabs behind the main building. On my way down Mill Street I passed the gates of the Avenue. The trees stood out against the sky and they were bare like women's arms. I remembered Binty telling us the legend of the red woman when the fire at the Banks made bright tiles in Deeds glasses and when Binty got to the strangling part Deeds reached long fingers towards Jammy's throat and we all laughed.

The Harbour cafe was ready to close when I got there. Chairs were stacked on tables. I cleared one table and sat down. No one came near me. The woman who owned the cafe came out to put the closed sign on the door and dim the lights.

78

She didn't look in my direction. She went back into the kitchen and I heard her talking about how Deeds had stabbed Glennon in the Plant and then had gone to the Glennon house with a petrol bomb. The way she talked you knew she couldn't wait to get home and draw the curtains.

The frame of the poolroom door held the darkness inside. At first I thought the breathless noises I could hear were voices from the poolroom and for a moment I was aware of all the shadows around me. Then I looked up and saw Anne-Marie standing in front of me with a cup of tea in her hand and I knew that I had heard her walking between the tables, the blue and white checked nylon of her apron rustling.

She reached out to put the cup in front of me. I could see moisture on her forearm and hand under the small hairs. The skin was white and the muscle on her arm was rounded. You imagined that it would be warm to touch even though it looked bloodless. The cup shifted on the saucer as she put it down. She lifted another chair and sat down opposite me.

The tea grew cold. The owner left, shouting out in the darkness for Anne-Marie to lock up. We didn't speak. Her breathing was regular and deep as if she was asleep but her eyes were open and she seemed to be looking over my shoulder the way any woman looks over your shoulder when she is alone in the dark listening to the noise you make on top of her. We waited. As if we were all waiting. Sharon for her brief language, Deeds and Jammy for wings sifting the air and the soft sounds birds made to themselves, Binty for silk parachutes falling to earth and the click of heels across the beach.

Anne-Marie took my cup and saucer to the kitchen. When she came back she lifted both chairs onto the table. Outside she put a key in the lock and turned it. We walked down the Harbour road towards the Banks.

There were no formalities with her. You walked in silence until you found a spot and then you lay down. Once she got into her stride you knew that you might as well be anyone. It was almost as if you could get up and walk away and she would still be lying there, her eyes closed and her soft, little mouth probing the night air like the snout of some half-blind night creature.

We were on a patch of grass half-way down the cliff path. If

79

you looked up you could see the lights of the Harbour reflected on the underside of the low cloud making the night seem twice as dark and full of flame.

Suddenly I remembered one of the pictures that Deeds had torn from a porn magazine and stuck to the wall of the loft. It showed a tomb in Paris. The man had been the founder of a fertility cult, Deeds told me, and the place was still a shrine. He was cast in bronze, lying on his back in a frock coat and top hat. The girl in the photograph wore a black veil. She had hitched up her black dress and straddled the lying figure, crushing her pink genitals against the bronze crotch.

I opened my eyes and saw that Anne-Marie's eyes were open and staring over my shoulder at the spot where I had last talked with Deeds. I felt a chill run through me and forced her eyes to mine and kissed them and kissed them again because as far as I was concerned there were no beautiful strangers and the only ghosts in this town are the ones that are walking the streets.

STORIES

THE LION ALONE

The sky over Tigers Bay was as dull as milk. It was overcast and warm. It had been warm for a week and the smell of rotting horseflesh and lion shit greased the rust-coloured bricks of the houses, draped the telephone wires, and threaded fingers of odour in the crudely-welded wire mesh that covered the windows of the shop on the corner.

Gus Ferguson emerged from the shop clutching two comics and a sherbet dip. Ignoring the smell he opened a comic on the windowsill of the shop and dipped the liquorice stick into the sherbet. The jungle doctor, he read, gunned his zebra-striped jeep through the bush. It was a race against time, but the jungle doctor braked hard and gaped in awe as the apeman swung himself, hand over hand, to the top of the tallest tree in the continent. Shading his eyes Gus Ferguson looked up at the towering gantry of the shipyard crane behind the houses. The apeman roared and pounded his chest.

Because of the smell Mrs Dorcas Wilson from No 72 had opened the telephone directory and noted the numbers of the police and the city zoo.

But the smell did not concern the lion for in the endless eye of his mind all was lion. The smell, the man who brought his meat, the ten feet by ten feet square of yard where he was lion and lion alone, the street, the city, the sky were endless lion without horizon, the pap of its bones.

Buck Spence worked on the docks. He was a timid man who had kept a lion in his back yard for so many years its origin had been forgotten. Perhaps it had come on one of the big African freighters, their holds dreaming with the green weight of African bananas.

Every Saturday morning an abbatoir van would halt at the kerb in front of No 70. The driver wore white oilskins. Buck Spence helped him to unload slabs of horsemeat which

83

they would shoulder and carry down the narrow corridor which led from the front of No 70 to the rear, piling them in a corner of the back kitchen. As they worked Buck Spence complained about the weight, or the price, or the blood which ran from the larded sides of meat, congealing the fibres of the carpet into bristles.

Every Saturday afternoon Buck Spence walked the lion to the corner of the street and back, his head almost level with the undulant joint of the lion's shoulder, the reflection of the street held in the great mongoose circle of the lion's eye. Every Saturday afternoon Mrs Dorcas Wilson watched them with increasing bitterness. She did not hold with lions. Her yard was separated from Buck Spence's yard by a wall of breezeblocks topped with a wire mesh fence. She had tolerated lion hairs which penetrated the fence and were carried into the house to irritate her husband's allergy, but this time things had gone too far.

Despite the heat she put on the tweed coat with the leather buttons before stepping into the street to knock on the door of No 70.

Buck Spence opened the door. At his back the smell from the corridor loomed, a roar of blood and gristle.

— You have my heart scalded with the smell of that bloody cat, she told him.

— The smell's terrible, Buck Spence agreed, and he has me eaten out of house and home.

— My Wilfred is distracted with it, she went on, disconcerted, the whole street thinks your head is cut.

— My head must be cut, he concurred gloomily, lions is unpredictable. One blow of a paw would gut you. I'm living in constant danger.

Mrs Dorcas Wilson's mouth, slotted with age, tightened under the stress until she was gilled like a fish. She shook her finger in Buck Spence's face until the knuckle rattled inside the hollow flesh like dice in a cup.

— I'll not be responsible, she warned.

Gus Ferguson turned the pages of the comic, his fingers sticky in the afternoon heat. In the yard of No 70 the lion yawned a watering-hole yawn and stood to unleash a dusty stream of lion's piss. Tigers Bay stank like the ribcage of a half-eaten beast on a plain without shade or mercy.

Mrs Dorcas Wilson sat by the window.

— I'm foundered, she told her husband, that damn Ferguson boy is hanging about the shop again. He should be in school.

— It's Saturday, Wilfred said, without taking his eyes from the television.

Mrs Dorcas Wilson watched Fiona Taggart from No 80 walk down the street, her brown breasts bobbing adams-apple tight against her chest.

— The cut of her, Mrs Dorcas Wilson snapped, it's enough to drive a body wild.

It was warm. Buck Spence dragged a sweating carcass from the pile in the back kitchen and pushed it through the back door. He listened for a moment to moist scuffles and devout grunts, sighed, then went into the front kitchen where he took the tea caddy from the shelf. Under a framed print of Isambard Kingdom Brunel Buck Spence began to make tea.

It was ominously quiet outside the compound, Gus Ferguson read. There had never been so many blossoms on the Frangipani. The dustbowl that surrounded the tiny compound was empty but soon it would be swarming with endless spears and he had only a handful of men. He composed himself to write a letter to his wife.

At exactly half past four Buck Spence and the lion left No 70, walked to the end of the street, turned and came back. Mrs Dorcas Wilson reached for the telephone.

At six o clock a police landrover entered Tigers Bay and parked at the kerb opposite No 70. Shortly afterwards a small, white van pulled up behind the landrover. A policeman walked from the landrover to the van and talked to the driver, then the driver and the policeman walked to the door of No 70. Fiona Taggart came to the doorway of No 80. When she saw the policeman her mouth made an O as round and brown as the brown egg breasts basketed against her chest.

— Gawking at a peeler, the scut, Mrs Dorcas Wilson said, smacking her lips.

When Buck Spence answered the door the vandriver stepped forward.

— Are you the boy that has the lion? he asked.

— That's who I am, Buck Spence said in a small voice, the

85

boy who has the lion.

— Have you the licence? the vandriver asked.

— Damn the licence he has, Mrs Dorcas Wilson said from the doorway of No 72.

— Wilful possession of a wild beast without a licence is an offence under section 30 (c) of the act, the vandriver said, making a note on a clipboard.

— Nobody told me, Buck Spence said.

— And a public nuisance, the policeman said.

— Nuisance is not the word, Mrs Dorcas Wilson said.

— It's a bloody menagerie, the policeman said.

— I was called out once to a case where a man kept a vulture in his living-room, the vandriver said as he walked back towards the van, a bird of carrion.

He returned with a rifle. He patted the barrel.

— .22 loaded with a hypodermic shot. Hit them anywhere in the body and over they go, out for the count. Accurate up to a hundred yards.

— Sterling sub-machine gun, standard issue, the policeman said, holding up his gun, a hundred rounds a minute. Not accurate though. It sprays bullets.

— Right, the vandriver said, slipping off the safety catch, let's go.

He led the way down the narrow corridor followed by the policeman, then Mrs Dorcas Wilson, then Gus Ferguson, then Buck Spence.

Ten minutes later they emerged in reverse order. No-one spoke. The policeman looked thoughtful.

The vandriver broke the silence.

— You didn't have to shoot it.

— It was about to spring at your throat, the policeman said.

— It was yawning, Gus Ferguson said.

The vandriver snapped open the rifle and removed the hypodermic cartridge.

— I could sue, Buck Spence said. The policeman looked at Buck Spence, then looked at Gus Ferguson.

— Children, he said, were at risk. And he went to the landrover to fetch chalk so that he could draw an outline of the dead lion on the concrete surface of the yard. When that was done he helped the vandriver to drag the body of the lion down the narrow corridor. The corpse was put in the back of the small white van and they drove off. Gus Ferguson ran after them as far as the corner.

— Good bloody riddance, Mrs Dorcas Wilson said, and closed the door of No 72.

— Eaten out of house and home, Buck Spence said, but the street was empty.

Mrs Dorcas Wilson cooked tea for Wilfred. Rashers lean and dark, sausages plump, fried bread and eggs. Wilfred ate slowly, with little relish. When he left the table Mrs Dorcas Wilson gathered the scraps carefully. Salty rinds and one fat sausage, stowed and wrapped in a handkerchief.

Slowly she went up the stairs. At a certain point where the wall was thin she stooped to listen but there was no sound from No 70. She went into the bathroom at the top of the stairs, closed and locked the door carefully behind her.

The book from the library had said that alligators preferred to eat meat that they had killed themselves but gradually she had persuaded him to accept household scraps. He almost filled the bath now, measuring five feet from the pointed tip of his snout to the end of his scaly tail. His stillness was immeasurable until he opened his mouth to receive the scraps.

The street had cooled a little at nightfall. Fiona Taggart, dressed to kill, left her house and saw a pampas moon. Two salamanders waited without noise in the shadow of a chimney. A fruit-eating bat gobbled a squashed tomatoe in the gutter outside the shop. Fiona Taggart began to walk towards the city and as she walked the hard, brown meat of her breasts whispered. On the distant shoulder of Cavehill mountain the wolves answered with their craving silence.

LOVE IN HISTORY

Sergeant Gabriel Hooper had a kodak monochrome photograph of Betty Grable on the wall of his room. In the photograph she was sitting astride the barrel of an anti-aircraft gun. Her skin was white and her black lips were drawn back from her teeth in a smile which captured the light of an entire aircraft carrier.

If you pulled down the top of Betty Grable's swimming costume the breasts underneath would be white, shaved cones like pencils with exact graphite tips.

In 1945 the uniform crotches of USAAF pilots were stiff with beauty.

Sergeant Gabriel Hooper had been stationed in RAF Cranfield since 1942. His billet was in an old house beside the seven salty miles of the runway. Sand blown up from the beach piled against the seaward gable wall. New hangars creaked in derelict breezes, and the red singing tongue of a windsock pointed towards Russian Winters and Tripoli landings.

At night he sat on his bed in USAAF shorts and singlet writing letters to his wife in handwriting which seemed like some complicated calculation of crosswinds and velocity over target. Somewhere in Kansas or Oklahoma was a dusty mailbox crammed with letters which his wife never answered.

In the bedroom of 1945 Adelene fastened the catch of her brassiere around her waist and twisted its stiff points upwards and around to put it into place. With a sweater over the top her breasts were like the tops of pencils, her black hair was a replica in lacquer, her white thighs stormed the map of the heart.

During the day Adelene counted cellophane packets of American stockings and ate American peaches from the tin with her fingers. At night pilots held her against the

88

perimeter fence, flattening her breasts against their tunic pockets. When she took a job in the aerodrome canteen she adjusted her mouth with lipstick using the polished tea-urn as a mirror in which pilots returning from missions looked for her mouth, lurid with desire or grief.

When Gabriel Hooper saw her there for the first time he thought of Betty Grable. Then he thought of his wife's kiss, the light, sour touch of her lips like sweat drying between the shoulderblades. He looked down at his blue-veined hands and they trembled like the ancient stained-glass of cathedrals in Dresden or Coventry.

Gabriel Hooper kept a photograph of himself and his wife in his breast pocket. The pocket of a dead pilot is often found to contain a rabbit's foot, or photobooth snapshot from a port entrance or railway station or other point of departure.

In the photograph Gabriel Hooper was sitting in a deckchair. Behind him was a water tower and beyond that grass stretched towards a monotone skyline. His wife sat between his legs, looking into the sun, expressionless as a woman of Europe, deprived of time and place to mourn.

Each Saturday night a truck left the airfield for the town. The truck brought aircrews to the Aurora cinema, or the Central ballroom, or the Island cafe. Tonight Gabriel Hooper was sitting under the canvas flaps beside the tailgate where he could see bombers practising night-landings at the far end of the runway, the red flares of their exhausts like islands burning in a smoky archipelago across the Pacific.

Adelene heard the bombers from her bedroom. She looked into the mirror with the brown tip of a hairpin between her lips and thought about the incendiary sky over Dresden terrible with white pearls of men's flesh.

When the truck pulled up outside the Central ballroom the street was busy with men in uniform, their pockets full of Fanny Mae's toffees, razor blades and silk stockings. They were watched ravenously from windows and mirrors by thousands of women with red lips and starved fox-fur collars.

Beside the glass box office of the Aurora cinema was a full-length poster of Betty Grable. On the steps of the Central ballroom two military policemen beat a black serviceman with batons. When he looked up his mouth was a red rose.

Inside the ballroom Gabriel Hooper watched Adelene

dance in arms that smelt of Palmolive. Gabriel Hooper watched her with such intensity that his eyes could have pierced immeasurable distances of war and desolation to reach the exact spot under the left breast where Betty Grable's monochrome heart pumped Pearl Harbour, or Omaha Beach through paper veins. He drew a Lucky Strike from the packet and tapped unanswerable signals with the tip of the cigarette on the lid of the packet.

She watched him approach in the mirrored lid of a powder compact. When he asked her to dance she answered yes and he smiled the wide, blue smile of a drought in the cornbelt.

I never seen you before, she said, close to his ear. I never noticed you in the canteen. I never seen you drunk like the others. I never seen you playing baseball behind the hangars, or dancing like a flag in white USAAF shorts with the other men when they swim on the beach, standing waistdeep in the water or floating on their backs smoking like Daily Mail photographs of endless husbands floating in the shallow, oily waters of Dunkirk.

I've seen you before, he said. I've seen your red lips in the canteen after a late shift as I lay awake and alone. I've heard you laugh with men as I lay alone when the sound of a wife's kiss is the sound of Betty Grable's heart broken with frost in the night.

Fancy a drink? she said, I'm parched. They went to the balcony. He fetched two cups of tea. Do you miss home? she asked. Are you homesick?

How many in your family? Are you married? He held out the photograph of his wife and himself mutely, as if they were the victims of an accident, without mentioning dates of birth, or the name of a town in Kansas or Oklahoma. Lovely, Adelene said, is that you?

When Adelene went to the toilet Gabriel Hooper looked again at his own face and his wife's face, dazzled by sunlight on zinc barns, and rainless seasons of drought and dustbowl politics. He lowered the tip of his cigarette to his wife's face and inhaled the moist, chemical smell of burnt Kodak.

Outside she slipped her arm through his. They walked out of town until they reached the perimeter fence of the aerodrome. What's your wife's name? she asked. Cissy, he said. It was the sound that sand from the beach made when the wind carried it across concrete.

Do you think I look like Betty Grable? she asked, they say I'm the dead spit of her. Wait till you see.

She put her back against one of the fence posts and raised her face so that her throat was visible, and he could see, like the faces of an audience, white porcelain insulators on telegraph poles.

Have you got a rabbit's foot? she asked. He nodded. Where? He touched the outside of his trouser pocket lightly. Her hand travelled past a handkerchief, a stub of pencil, coins and a brass Zippo to the shreds of tobacco in the pocket lining where there was a soft foot the size of a lost button and he smiled at the memory of a rabbit surprised in the open on the yellow grass of Kansas or Oklahoma.

Gabriel Hooper woke at dawn and walked naked to the window. In the distance rain scratched the tin roofs of Nissan huts and hangars. Driven inland by an advancing frontal system seagulls squatted at the edge of the wet, black runway. Behind him Adelene turned in her sleep and the sheets crackled like parachute silk drifting over cornfield or open sea.

A wife's name is the sound that sand makes when the wind carries it across concrete. A wife's kiss is the sound of Betty Grable's heart broken with frost in the night. Gabriel Hooper walked naked to the window to look for America but it was lost in an advancing frontal system, weather in which men find themselves mapless and bereft.

If you pull down the top of Betty Grable's swimming costume her breasts are as smooth as the cone of a navigator's unreliable pencil. If you pull down the top of her swimming costume her breasts accuse and her navel is like a spotlight scanning the skyline of Europe for love in history, finding you then losing you between gaps in the clouds.

RADIO 1974

Creed recognised her voice because he had heard it on the radio fifteen years ago. He imagined the earpiece of the phone pushed under her blond hair and her lips speaking. She did not apologise for ringing and she used his father's first name.

The crisis came at 1.03 a.m. JJ didn't wake but the nurse saw him convulse, the right hand with the long yellow fingers rising slowly from the pillow, the arm also rising then collapsing in a spasm as a scrap of paper will collapse when burning. His black fringe fell over his eyes.

First there was a wind and then rain. Creed drove for an hour through small towns where the wind blew grit along the pavements and the lit shop windows seemed empty, their shelves gathering dust. After that the road passed between trees which strained as if they were being sucked upwards by the wind. Gale warning, the radio said. Dogger bank, Cromertie, Forties.

The telephone had made her voice sound exactly the way it had sounded on the radio fifteen years before. Are you aware of JJ's condition? she asked. I haven't seen or spoken to my father for fifteen years, he said. They don't know how long he's got, she said, I'll stay away tonight if you want to see him.

In 1974 JJ had brought home a piece of sandpaper found in the street after a bomb. Smell it, he said. It smelt of marzipan and Creed had thought about raisins, chopped almonds, orange peel. That's gelignite, JJ said.

It was nine o'clock when he got to the hospital and the rain was blowing lean and horizontal across the carpark.

He went to the reception desk and the duty nurse checked the register. He followed another nurse to the ward. Her rubber-soled shoes hummed on the oily, polished floor. Her linen skirt made a clean rattle against the back of her knees.

Somewhere in this hospital there were stiff rows of those uniforms hanging on pegs and nurses dressing. Just a minute. A dab of perfume between the breasts. Ready sister.

The nurse nodded to him and pointed. Room 203. The door was ajar. Creed pushed it and saw JJ lying on the bed, the blanket pushed back and his knees tucked towards his chest. The hospital gown did not meet properly at the back so that he could see all the way down his father's spine to the grinning, white moth of his buttocks. He used to lie in the bath like that, reading a paperback, a cigarette dissolving in the soapdish.

I shouldn't be here. It should be Angela Doherty with her blonde hair that would wrap you better than a hospital gown as you lay dying. I am no more help than the ashtray on the bedside locker. Than the yellow Sanyo face of the radio beside it that stares at the back of your sleeping head.

He sat on the metal-framed chair beside the bed and lit a cigarette. History is a river, you used to say, and your river started for me when you told me how you once climbed out of a bedroom window and walked down the street to watch a house on fire. It was snowing. The snow fell into the fire and the boy's bare feet blazed in the snow. The flame crept up through his body to light the folded touchpaper of pneumonia in his lungs.

Didn't stop you smoking though. You always had long yellow fingers from smoking. Long, thieving fingers. He looked into his father's face. The stubble was gray in places. The hair in each nostril was gray. Where are you daddy? Are you in the long corridor with the years opening off it, wondering which one will you hide in next? Don't go into 1974. I'm in there.

You have a long record of disbelieved histories. Did you ever really have pneumonia? When I was old enough to be a boy in the snow I asked you what you did during the war and you said you were in the secret service and that you were part of a team that made a battleship disappear behind a secret forcefield.

A secret forcefield. Now that's privacy for you, deeper than sleep. My daddy's ship was anchored behind a secret forcefield in 1942.

In 1974 a Unionist walked onto the balcony of Stormont

castle in the Province of Ulster to announce the beginning of the Ulster Workers' strike. We listened to him on the radio. Hearing the broken veins that started at the corner of his nose and spread onto his cheeks. Hearing the people beneath the balcony pointing flags, microphones and placards while we sat at home and listened and pointed the silence which was the only thing we had to point with.

Creed had thought that refugees were people in muddy straw hats walking on a road which is raised between rice fields. Smoke rises from the city behind them and no-one looks back. But everyone finds their own refuge and that night the power stations began to close and Catholic cars began to stream south so that in the darkness it looked as if all the light in Northern Ireland had been imprisoned in cars and driven indefinitely across the border.

However the veins on your nose were not broken by history and your skin is not yellow because of it. The day you left us I asked you where you were going and you said you were going to a secret conference on the future of the North. When you didn't come back I found a photograph of her in the back of a wallet you left behind. Her two lips confer with yours.

At least she got you a private room. Matt blue with soft fluorescent lights. No windows but by the look of you you're not going to have any more need of windows. You can die in the dark as well as any other way if it comes to it. My mother did, but that was after you left. Without aid or succour of daylight.

Your lips are moving as you sleep JJ. My mother said that you began to fox sleep before you left so that you could avoid talking, or explaining. Foxing sleep in the henhouse of her mind.

Your sleeping lips are saying that you were never a member of the secret service and that you never went to secret meetings on the future of the North.

I have a photograph of a civil rights meeting. You were still a history teacher when the photograph was taken. That could be you standing on the windy platform with the big ears and the fringe hanging over your eyes, hiding them so I can't see if that is the moment when you first smelt the exotic aroma of 1969, 1970, 1971, 1972, 1973 and 1974 and Burntollet and Reginald Maudling and Free Derry, bloody Sunday, bloody this, bloody that.

You met Angela Doherty at one of those meetings. Afterwards you sat in a pub, smoking and telling her that history is a river.

You took her to my mother's funeral and no-one spoke. She was wearing a black poloneck with a white miniskirt and white knee-length boots. I watched her and wondered why you had left us and gone with her. I hope that it was the aroma that led you there. That you came like a cannon on the walls of Derry and made the tear-gas and blood flow from her blue eyes.

But if I woke you you'd probably tell me that she was in the secret service as well.

Are you frightened now that the river has carried you past her into the dark estuary? If I wake you the estuary of your eye will be yellow with liver damage. The river of your eye flooded with unnavigable disease.

I will not wake you now. I will let you sleep because for all your secret service and secret meetings you were as frightened as the rest of us that day you took us out of school and put us in your car and followed all the rest of them across the border on the day during the strike when Harold Wilson, Prime Minister of Great Britain and Northern Ireland was to speak on television and radio the words that would send troops against the strikers.

Creed extinguished his last cigarette. As he walked back along the corridor he remembered Angela Doherty's voice of protest on the radio in 1974. History is a river, she said, and he had turned to look at his mother.

Outside the hospital the rain had stopped but the wind tugged at the steering of the car and the trees on either side of the road moved wildly as if some huge, shambling thing was forcing its way through the branches.

He turned on the radio and the nurse called a doctor who noted 1.03 am as being the time of death.

They had crossed the border that day and driven south until evening. They stopped on a quiet road because the car radio would not work when the car was moving. His father searched the dial for Harold Wilson's voice.

Spongers, Harold Wilson called the strikers, living off the British taxpayer. They listened to the broadcast and when it

95

was over his father turned it off and sat back so that there was silence for a moment. Although it was not yet dark Creed could see white moths moving in the ditches at either side of the road.

Wilson's given in, JJ said, he's backed down to the bastards. Does that mean we can go home? his mother asked.

And as he drove away from the hospital Creed wondered at how much it cost to turn and walk against the stream of refugees. Even for a moment to turn back and walk towards the flames of a city, and the silence therein.